MALCOLM MAHR

THE BOY WITH A PIPE

A NOVEL

This is a work of fiction. Some names, characters, places, and incidents are either the product of the author's imagination or are used fictitiously.

Any resemblance to actual persons, living or dead, events, or locales is entirely coincidental.

TREASURE
COAST
PRESS

Vero Beach, FL 32967
TCP27@aol.com

ISBN:978-0-692-19751-6
Printed in the United States of America

For Fran
More than ever

Also by Malcolm Mahr

FICTION

Featuring Frank Fernandez
No Man's Land
The Golden Madonna
The Hostage
The Einstein Project
The Orange Blossom Mob
Sandbag Castle

The Return of the Scorpion
The Secret Diary of Marco Polo
Murder at the Paradise Spa
The DaVinci Deception

NONFICTION

How to Win in the Yellow Pages
What Makes a Marriage Work
You're Retired Now. Relax.

The Boy With A Pipe

A NOVEL

"Bad artists copy; good artists steal."

—Pablo Picasso

PART I

THE STORM

"Irma is wider than our entire state. Do not ignore evacuation orders. Once the storm starts, law enforcement cannot save you."

—Florida Governor Rick Scott, September 7, 2017

...1

"THE DEAD MAN WAS DISCOVERED Monday, September 11th, 2017, south of the Navy SEAL Museum on North Hutchinson Island," Fort Pierce officials said.

Shortly before two p.m. a Hurricane Irma cleanup crew working in a tangle of waist-high sea oats and blown-over banyans discovered a body on the beach. The victim was taken to the medical examiner's office to establish identity and cause of death.

Officials said it was too early to determine if the fatality was a result of Hurricane Irma. Police asked anyone who had a loved one missing to contact them.

...2

"THAT DAMN HURRICANE was a pisser," said former Fort Pierce police chief Lou Brumberg. "According to the National Weather Service, we got the most rain in the state—twenty inches in some places." He sounded out of breath. "Just checking up on you, Frank. How did you and your family make out?"

"Maris and Charlie spent two nights in a shelter in St. Petersburg."

Fernandez knew that Hurricane Irma wasn't the reason for the call. Since Brumberg's retirement, the two men had had a strained relationship. One year earlier, Fernandez had investigated the stabbing death of an elderly Korean War veteran. The victim, Earle Mayfield, had been an Army officer responsible for authorizing the shooting and killing of innocent Korean refugees at the Pukhan River in 1951.

Fernandez had solved the murder, but because of the current political situation in Korea, the government had pressured him to refrain from exposing the atrocity. Fernandez had kept the chief of police out of the loop, which made Brumberg appear inept and triggered his retirement.

An awkward silence opened between the two men.

"And how's your 'whatchamacallit' therapy?" Brumberg asked.

"Chelaton."

"Yeah. How's that coming?"

"Lou," Fernandez said slowly. "What do you want?"

"Can't a friend call after a major hurricane to see how you're doing?"

"In your case, no. We haven't spoken in almost a year. All of a sudden you're interested in my health? Tell me why you called."

"I have a … situation that could be a win-win for us both."

"No thanks."

"At least hear me out, Frank."

Fernandez drew a heavy breath; he let it out. "Go on."

"I had time on my hands and took on the shit job of president of our condo in Ocean Village. These old biddies call me at all hours to fix their fucking disposals, clogged sinks and TVs. They bitch when somebody's not picking up dog shit and complain that the lobby furniture is a disgrace."

"Cut to the chase, Lou. Why did you call me?"

"During the hurricane, there was a robbery in one of our penthouse apartments. The owner is a lady named Grace Carlyle. She and her daughter discovered the theft when the power came on and they returned. Naturally she came to me for help.

"I told Mrs. Carlyle to report the robbery to the police and notify her insurance company. She couldn't get through to either one. I tried to contact my replacement; her name's Beauvoir. My calls weren't returned. Everybody was busy with storm-related issues. I was chief. I understand. Hell, the department was short-staffed even before the hurricane. And on top of that, a cleanup crew found a dead body on Pepper Beach."

"Why did you call, Lou?" Fernandez repeated.

"The lady's break-in was put on a back burner. I mentioned to her I knew an ex-FBI agent who was a private investigator and might be available to help her. She jumped at the idea. If you're interested, give her a call."

"Thanks, but why are you doing this?"

"I figured you could use the money."

"And the real reason, Lou?"

"To get the old biddy off my ass."

Fernandez wanted to say no. He felt partly responsible for the man losing his job. Fernandez also sensed the ex-police chief was lying—he wondered why.

...3

IT WAS LATE AFTERNOON by the time Fernandez worked out arrangements with Chief Beauvoir. He scheduled a five p.m. appointment with Mrs. Carlyle. Most break-ins amounted to filing a police report, examining surfaces for latent fingerprints, and helping the victims prepare insurance claims.

Fernandez drove across the Indian River Bridge to South Hutchinson Island. Seagulls squawked, rising and falling with the wind.

Slivers of heat lightning quivered on the horizon. A thread of sunlight broke through the heavy skies. Rain was on the way. Fernandez had an internal weather radar system: two little pieces of lead rattling around inside his chest, a time bomb surgeons couldn't remove.

During his last six-month checkup, Dr. Layton had arranged two X-rays on an illuminator.

"The one on the left was taken six months ago, when you finished chelaton therapy." He arranged the second X-ray directly over the first. The X-rays merged, similar in every detail except for a white speck circled on each plate.

"We never know when metal fragments stop or move," Dr. Layton said. "Shrapnel emerges from war veterans after fifty years."

"What are you telling me?"

"The particles are dangerously near your heart. I urge you to avoid physical exertion."

* * *

THE OCEAN VILLAGE GATEHOUSE was one mile south of the Fort Pierce Inlet on A1A. "I have an appointment," Fernandez said to the flat-nosed security guard. "Mrs. Carlyle in Seascape II."

"Photo I.D., please?"

The guard studied the card. "I'm Wayne Gibson. I remember you. You're Miss Vesta's boss, right?"

"That's debatable."

"I used to sing with her Avenue D Choir. How's Vesta?"

"Fine. The choir is performing at Disney World this week."

Fernandez slipped him a folded twenty-dollar bill.

"Couple of questions?"

The guard paused to wave a car through the right-hand lane.

"Were you on duty during the hurricane?"

"Until five o'clock Friday. Then we were relieved to look after our own families."

"Were the gates closed when you left?"

"That's standard procedure before a big blow. We took the arms off the gates and boarded the gatehouse."

"When did your guys come back on duty?"

"My shift returned Monday—to prevent looting."

"When did the power go on?"

"Wednesday. Then residents started drifting back."

"Much damage?"

"Dune erosion. That's all. We were lucky."

"You heard about the break-in?"

"Who hasn't?"

"Any idea how it could have happened, Wayne?"

"Both Indian River bridges were closed and guarded; no power in buildings; elevators on lockdown; mandatory evacuation; hundred-mile wind gusts; and flooded roads." Gibson grimaced and held his nose. "Something doesn't smell right."

Fernandez handed him his card. "If you think of anything, call me."

* * *

A TALL WOMAN who looked to be fifty-something greeted Fernandez at the penthouse.

"I'm Barbara McCuskey, Mrs. Carlyle's daughter."

Her expression was guarded as she apprised the olive-complexioned man standing in the doorway wearing clothes that looked like he had slept in them.

"You're here about the robbery?"

"Yes, ma'am. My name is Fernandez."

"This way, please."

Fernandez was aware of her musky scent and strikingly appealing body. He felt sudden warmth in his groin.

The living room was located directly off the foyer: Persian carpets, gold-framed paintings, an antique drop-front bureau, and drapes drawn against the harsh afternoon sun. Fernandez thought the unifying decorative theme was that everything cost a lot of money.

A small brown and white dog lay dozing on the sofa. Spotting Fernandez, the aged but still feisty spaniel growled energetically.

"Barbara, put Bentley in the den and close the door," said a sharp-nosed woman with a thin, patrician face and iron gray hair. "Bentley's never liked strangers," she said indifferently.

"He bit my husband once," volunteered Barbara.

"Yes, pity," her mother added, with an edge to her voice. "Pity it wasn't fatal."

There was a charged pause.

Barbara McCuskey's uneasiness was palpable.

"Mother, this is Mr. Fernandez. He's here about the robbery."

Hearing his Hispanic name, the woman blinked a couple of times. "Fernandez?" she repeated, with a trace of a southern accent. "Are you Mexican? That's what I want to know."

"Yes. My day job is a leaf-blower. I do investigations at night."

"I find that comment disrespectful," she sniffed.

Fernandez cleared his throat. "Let's get something straight. I offered to help as a favor to Mr. Brumberg. The police aren't staffed to investigate break-ins while they're investigating hurricane-related deaths."

Grace Carlyle narrowed her eyes. "Deaths?"

"One elderly couple died from asphyxiation due to a faulty generator. Neighbors called 9-1-1, but the fire district couldn't respond in time because of Irma's high winds. And a man was found dead on Pepper Beach."

Grace Carlyle gave a resigned sigh and gripped Fernandez's arm. "Understand, young man. I feel violated having my jewelry stolen."

"I'll do my best. That's all I can promise. Do you have a list of the missing items?"

Barbara McCuskey rummaged through the drop-front bureau. "Will this do?"

DECEMBER 15, 2013

APPRAISAL REPORT FOR INSURANCE
CATEGORY: JEWELRY

ITEM NO: 40-0001
APPRAISED: ONE W/G NECKLACE CONT. 1 PEAR- SHAPED OPAL, WEIGHING 921/100 AND 29 DIAS, TW 11 3/100 with W/G CHAIN: $2,400.00

ITEM NO: 40-0002
APPRAISED: ONE LADIES' WATCH, FREDERICK CONSTANT —NEIMAN-MARCUS: $9,995.00

ITEM NO: 40-0003
APPRAISED: ONE 3.59 KARAT E VVSI ROUND DIAMOND SOLITARE RING: $9,213.00

ITEM NO: 40-0004
APPRAISED: ONE STAMPED 14K WHITE DIAMOND ENGAGEMENT RING, ROW OF DIAMONDS SET DOWN THE RAISED SHANK ON EACH SIDE OF THE CENTER DIAMOND, WHICH IS SET INTO 4-PRONGS IN A 10.85 MM ROUND FRAME OF DIAMONDS: $10,400.00

ITEM NO: 40-0005
APPRAISED: MAN'S ROLEX STAINLESS STEEL/18 KARAT YELLOW GOLD BEZEL: $10,900.00

ITEM NO: 40-0006
APPRAISED: ONE PAIR OF DIAMOND EARRINGS, 17 KARAT WHITE GOLD, WEIGHING 3.81 DWT., EACH SET WITH A

ROUND BRILLIANT CUT DIAMOND IN A 6 PRONG HEAD: $35,700.00

TOTAL LISTED ITEMS: $78,608.00

Fernandez let out a low whistle. "Why keep valuables in your apartment rather than a safe deposit box?"

"It's a nuisance having Barbara run to the bank safe deposit box every time I want to wear something nice."

"I noticed an expensive man's watch on the list."

"That Rolex belonged to my first husband."

"Any storm damage?" he asked.

"No. Mother's windows were locked and shuttered."

Fernandez reached for a notebook and pen. He wanted Mrs. Carlyle to feel he was taking her seriously.

"Besides the jewelry, was anything else taken?"

"No," Barbara said.

"What about Anthony's painting?" Grace grumbled. "The one from the den that's missing."

"Mother. It was just a reproduction."

Fernandez looked confused. "Why would an intruder ignore valuable artwork hanging in plain sight and then take an inexpensive print? That makes no sense."

"Why aren't you checking for fingerprints?" Grace Carlyle demanded.

"At the present time, the crime lab is busy. But in my experience—"

She broke in. "Exactly what is your experience, young man?"

Fernandez bristled. "I was with the FBI for twenty years, then a private investigator for five years, and now they want me to teach criminal justice technology at Indian River State College. Any more questions?"

"I guess you'll do."

"Are you certain the missing print was hanging on the den wall before the storm?"

"I took a picture with my iPhone before we left."

"Please e-mail me a copy of the picture. Can you show me where the print was hanging?"

"In the den. Follow me."

Beneath a bare spot on the wall, Mrs. Carlyle's spaniel was gnawing on a sliver of plastic. Fernandez knelt, examining the blue scrap of plastic as Barbara McCuskey struggled to restrain the barking dog, stroking his fur, smoothing his ears.

"Marine shrink film," Fernandez observed. "Do you have a plastic baggie?"

With a pen, he transferred the film into the bag and rejoined Grace Carlyle and her daughter in the living room. Bentley was left in the den, growling and snarling.

"It's early in the investigation," Fernandez said. "No electronics were stolen, and the thieves had the foresight to bring waterproof plastic to cover the missing piece of artwork. I don't believe the break-in was a random heist by looters or druggies—the robbery required careful planning."

Mrs. Carlyle snapped, "Why in Heaven's name would they take a reproduction?"

"Very good question, ma'am. I'm wondering the same thing."

For the first time, Grace Carlyle allowed herself a smile. "Barbara, dear," she said. "Offer the nice gentleman some coffee."

Fernandez eyed a photograph on the piano of Grace and a suave-looking man with a salt-and-pepper mustache and a shaved head.

"Is that your husband?"

"My late husband. When my first husband died, it was a lonely time for me, and then I met Anthony. He was active in community affairs and president of the Vero Opera. Anthony took me dancing. He made me feel young again."

Barbara McCuskey returned with a tray of coffee. She listened for a few moments as her mother described Anthony Carlyle, and then she exhaled noisily and rolled her eyes heavenward.

Fernandez said, "I'd like to ask you a few more questions, Mrs. McCuskey."

Her glossy auburn hair was tied behind her, exposing the soft lines of her neck. There was a look of playful expectation in her eyes.

"Call me Barbara."

"Barbara. What time did you and your mother leave the apartment?"

"I guess it was about half-past five."

"Why didn't you take the jewelry with you?"

"Weather forecasters weren't certain where the hurricane would track. I felt it prudent to leave mother's jewelry in a locked apartment, in what was supposed to be a secure building, in a gated community."

"Understandable. And what were your hurricane preparations?"

"Lisa's crew secured the storm shutters and shut off the water."

"Who is Lisa?"

"Lisa Rodriguez has a cleaning service."

"What time were your cleaning people here?"

"Sometime after three p.m. I remember, because they shut the water off."

"Did you take the dog with you?"

"Lori is our dog walker. She boarded Bentley during the hurricane."

Fernandez jotted the information.

"What time did the dog walker pick up your mother's dog?"

"Around five o'clock, just before we left for Brad's daughter's house in Maitland. The guard helped with the suitcases and made sure the apartment was locked."

"You have a key lock?"

"No. We punch in combination numbers."

"Who besides you two knew the combination?"

"My husband, Brad; Lisa, the cleaning lady; and the dog walker."

Grace Carlyle snapped, "Also Stanley, the maintenance man."

"Barbara, was your husband here to help?"

Mrs. Carlyle grimaced at the mention of her daughter's husband. She made a dismissive gesture with her hand, as if brushing away a bug.

"Brad was shuttering our apartment and securing his boat."

"The security guard. Do you know his name?"

"I have no idea."

"Can you describe him?"

"Lanky fellow with bone-white hair, and he had a dreadful scar on his forehead."

Fernandez looked at his notes. "It would be helpful to talk to your maintenance man, the dog walker, the cleaning lady, and your husband. Please contact them and ask that they meet here at nine a.m. tomorrow."

Mrs. Carlyle grumbled. "Why bother these people?"

"Because I'm a pond man."

"A what?"

"An investigation is like a pond. Toss in a few pebbles and watch the ripples."

His cell phone rang. It was the medical examiner, Dr. Miriam Jolson.

"Get your sorry ass down to the police station, Frank," Jolson said.

* * *

As Fernandez drove past the gatehouse, he beckoned to Wayne Gibson.

"Wayne, what's the name of the guard who is middle-aged, white-haired and has a scar on his forehead?"

"Leroy Martin. He worked part-time. Leroy's day job was security at the art museum up in Vero."

"Was?"

"Leroy was found dead on Pepper Beach."

...4

THE FORT PIERCE POLICE STATION was a boxy, one-story brown building with a patch of satellite dishes and antenna sprouting from the roof. The three flagpoles stood tall and empty, a stark reminder of the recent damaging hurricane winds.

After being scanned by a metal detector, Fernandez was directed to the meeting room. At seven p.m., the new police chief addressed the investigative team. Garcella Beauvoir was in uniform, collar stars marking her rank. Beauvoir was a handsome woman in her early sixties, with a round face, a high forehead, honey-colored skin, and wispy gray among the black in her hair. Fernandez liked that. She wasn't trying to hide her age. He nodded to Miriam Jolson, the county medical examiner.

Detective Floyd Emerson lumbered in and sat in the back of the room. Emerson's thin, handsome face had gained more lines. He gave Fernandez a hard look.

Captain Beauvoir looked at her investigative team's exhausted faces. Some had worked through the storm with little or no sleep. The chief began by explaining what most people in the room already knew: a man had been found dead on North Hutchinson Island.

The chief stammered, "No f-footprints or fingerprints, and no witnesses have come forward. You wouldn't expect to find anybody of sound mind wandering on the b-beach in a category four hurricane. As of now, we have no suspects or people of interest. The victim's watch, wallet and cell phone were found at the scene."

Fernandez noticed a couple of detectives fold their arms and breathe out heavily, on the brink of yawning. He asked, "Were any credit cards stolen from the wallet?"

"Not that we know of." Beauvoir continued, "The cause of death was loss of blood as a result of traumatic injuries to his head, which the medical examiner will elaborate on shortly. Some organic matter found at the scene has been sent for DNA analysis. Hopefully, we will be getting the results shortly, but with the storm-related problems, that timing is problematic. Other potential evidence is being examined by forensics."

Fernandez realized that without the murder weapon, suspects, motive or witnesses—they had nothing.

Floyd Emerson stuck his hand up. "I have to ask you, *boss*." He pronounced the word with exaggerated slowness. "What's that has-been Fernandez doing here?"

Beauvoir's face turned a mottled red as Emerson looked around the room to gather support.

Fernandez was taken aback. His relationship with Emerson had been bumpy, but he'd never expected to be attacked publicly.

An uneasy silence engulfed the room.

Beauvoir started to stammer a response, when Medical Examiner Miriam Jolson stood up and faced the group. Jolson was in her early fifties, an attractive, fair-skinned lady with copper-colored hair. Unmarried, Jolson had served a tour in Afghanistan as a captain in the Florida National Guard. Fernandez knew she didn't suffer fools gladly.

"Knock it off, Emerson," Jolson said. "You people have a shitload of work ahead, and this department is short-staffed. I asked for Frank, and Chief Beauvoir approved.

Do you have a problem with that, Floyd, or are you just pissed off because you were passed over for police chief?"

Emerson looked down at his palms. He muttered something between his teeth.

Miriam Jolson continued, "The autopsy revealed a major skull fracture. The victim suffered two blows to the head with a blunt instrument. Either of the two blows could have been fatal. The weapon was heavy—perhaps a bat or piece of pipe—and as a result, the occipital bone was smashed. That's the trapezoidal-shaped bone at the lower-back area of the cranium. The murder weapon has not been recovered."

"Time of death?" one detective asked.

"The body wasn't found until after the storm had passed. Based on body temperature and rigor mortis, we believe the death occurred between six and eight p.m. Sunday night. I checked the victim's hands and knuckles and scraped his nails. There were no traces of a struggle."

"A question," Fernandez said. "Did the forensic examination of the point of impact indicate that the attacker was taller or shorter than the victim?"

"The downward blow was delivered by someone taller. Since the victim was five feet eleven inches, we can assume the killer was over six feet tall."

Beauvoir looked at her watch. "It's late. Go home, get some sleep, and let's start fresh tomorrow."

There was a collective sigh of relief.

"But listen up," she added. "Say nothing to reporters. Any media involvement right now will be an unwelcome distraction."

Miriam Jolson said to Fernandez, "Thanks for coming, Frank. If I preferred men, you would be on my A list." She kissed him on the cheek before she left.

As the room emptied, Floyd Emerson walked over and snickered. "I hear your old lady's coming back to Fort Pierce with her bastard—"

Fernandez's hand shot out and grabbed the detective's right index finger, forcing it back to the breaking point until Emerson grunted in pain. "Just messing with you," he croaked. "Jesus, man, let me go—you're crazy."

Garcella Beauvoir separated the two.

"Emerson." Her eyes narrowed into slits. "Your behavior tonight was unacceptable. If you can't handle working for a woman, I'll help you relocate."

Before Emerson could manage a reply, Beauvoir snapped, "That's all. You're dismissed." She turned to Fernandez and gave her head a tilt toward her office.

* * *

THE POLICE CHIEF'S OFFICE looked different from the last time Fernandez had been there. Instead of Brumberg's desk covered with papers, it was neat and tidy. The Navy SEAL trident wall clock was gone, as was the shriveled cactus on the windowsill. The wall corkboard was no longer a mass of multicolored Post-it Notes, and the visitors' chairs had been recovered in tan leather.

A painting on the wall captured Fernandez's attention. It was a disturbing scene with dead trees and people with sticks confronting a dark figure clutching a child.

"This is a painting entitled *Revenge*, by Rigaud Benoit," Garcella said. "Benoit is one of the great names in Haitian art."

"If you don't mind my saying so, it's creepy."

The police chief ignored his comment. "I'm new here, Mr. Fernandez. I realize people will be looking over my shoulder: Fort Pierce's first Haitian police chief, a female and all that nonsense."

"You might cut Emerson some slack," Fernandez said. "He's going through a messy divorce. Floyd can be a solid detective—when he wants to be."

She smiled, her eyes taking his measure. "I'll think about it."

Fernandez sensed what was coming next.

"Miriam Jolson said you were an experienced investigator. I'm short staffed and could use your help in investigating the murder case."

"Thanks for the offer, Chief. My answer is no. As a favor to Brumberg, I agreed to help with the Carlyle break-in. But for murder investigations, I'm over the hill."

Garcella offered him a thin smile. "I've heard it said, 'When you're over the hill, you begin to pick up speed.'"

"No, you begin to pick up arthritis and an enlarged prostate."

* * *

IT WAS AFTER TEN P.M. when Fernandez pulled into his condominium's parking lot. In the semi-darkness, he eyed an old man bent double, leaning on a cane. After the recent brutal murder in the building, residents were uneasy with strangers loitering in the parking area.

"Can I help you, sir? Are you lost?"

"Lost?" The man laughed a sad laugh. "A question that cannot be answered in a few words. If you're making reference to where I am destined, it is to my apartment. And who might you be, the night watchman?"

"My name is Fernandez. I live in the building."

They shook hands. Fernandez felt unexpected strength in the old man's grip.

"I'm Avram. Avram Markus. May I offer you coffee or a nightcap?"

It had been a long day. A drink would be welcome.

Markus turned his back and fumbled at the door before inserting the key.

Fernandez recognized the anti-surveillance protocol. His new neighbor was checking to see if anyone had broken in. He had probably attached scotch tape or a hair across the doorframe.

In the hallway light Fernandez observed his new neighbor. The old man had a common-looking face with heavy-lidded blue eyes, bushy eyebrows and a full head of hair, all white. He looked to be in his mid-seventies.

Who the hell is this guy?

*　*　*

THE LAST TIME FERNANDEZ had entered the apartment was when Earle Mayfield, the Korean veteran, was stabbed to death. Mayfield's unit had been repainted. The walls were bare, save for one painting.

The apartment was as sparsely furnished as a hotel room. A cracked tan leather sofa and a La-Z-Boy recliner were grouped in front of a television set. Books appeared to be Markus's only personal items. An unusual painting hung on the wall, a woman holding a child watching a man playing a violin.

"Coffee or brandy?"

"Brandy sounds good."

Avram shuffled into the kitchen. He reappeared with a cut-glass decanter filled with an amber-colored liquid.

"Metaxa from Greece; aged in oak."

The old man clinked glasses with a hand that wasn't quite steady. He intoned, "Give me, Lord, my daily bread … and I will get my own brandy." Markus made his brandy vanish in one swallow, with no grunting or throat clearing.

Fernandez took a cautious sip. The brandy had a spicy, orange flavor. He gulped the rest. It gave his heart a brief squeeze on the way down.

They drank for a moment in silence, and then Fernandez said, "I rented this apartment for my dad, but he decided against it."

"Why turn down such a nice unit?"

"My father suffered a heart attack. He's in a wheelchair. I wanted him to come to Florida. He hates cold weather. In the Korean War he survived the cold nightmare of Chosin Reservoir."

Markus tipped the decanter. "Another?"

Fernandez held up his empty glass. Marcus poured another measured serving.

"Dad's heart attack put a scare into him. He moved to an assisted living facility in Baltimore. My brother is a doctor at Johns Hopkins."

"Your father's illness is regrettable," Markus said. "But I'm pleased to have found this apartment. I was renting around the corner on Avenue D. The storm caused severe water damage, and the owner is waiting for insurance money before he starts repairs. By that time, he will have mold … and I will be dead."

Markus smiled and helped himself to another drink. "Do you have a family?"

The question gave Fernandez pause. "More or less." The Metaxa made him slightly light-headed. To his surprise, he began to talk about his situation.

"I have a son—and he's not mine, exactly. My wife managed the local Fort Pierce art museum. After a fire totally destroyed the gallery, Maris was out of a job. She was offered a position with the Dali Museum in St. Petersburg."

He sighed deeply. "One thing led to another, and we became estranged. Maris moved in with someone … and became pregnant." Fernandez drained his glass. "That was a couple of years back. She broke up with the guy, and now we are seeing each other again, trying to work things out."

"And the child?"

"Charlie is three years old."

Markus's smile faded. "You hold on to that little boy," he grunted.

"I intend to."

"Forgive me," Markus said, taking heavy, deep breaths. "Metaxa loosens an old fool's tongue." He changed the subject. "What do you do for a living, Mr. Fernandez?"

"I was in the FBI. Now I run a private investigating firm. How about you? What line of work were you in?"

Markus paused before answering. "I was in the … pest control business."

Fernandez stared into the old man's icy blue eyes.

"You were an exterminator?"

"You could call it that."

...5

AT NINE A.M., FERNANDEZ ENTERED Grace Carlyle's top floor apartment. Off to the east he could see the ocean shimmering. To the north he had a clear view of the Fort Pierce Inlet. To make the interviews less intimidating, he had brought along a box of Dunkin' Donuts.

Barbara McCuskey told him Bentley was being dog walked. He assumed the dog walker would be back in time to be interviewed.

"Thank you for coming," Fernandez said to the four people assembled in the living room. "I'm investigating a break-in that occurred during Hurricane Irma. Let me say that no one here is under suspicion. Otherwise we wouldn't be meeting in Mrs. Carlyle's apartment, eating doughnuts and drinking coffee."

"Beware of Greeks bearing gifts," Barbara McCuskey's husband chortled. The man was tall, tanned, in his sixties, and stylishly unshaven.

"I'm Hispanic, so you needn't worry."

A sprinkle of laughter followed.

"I plan to interview each of you separately."

Stanley Wilson, the maintenance man, spoke up. "I got a ton of things to do since the storm. If you could take me first, I'd much appreciate it."

Brad McCuskey checked his watch, shrugged, took two donuts and left the room.

Lisa Rodriguez said, "My cleaning crew is working in the building. Here's my cell number. When you're ready, give me a call."

* * *

"MR. WILSON," FERNANDEZ SAID to the maintenance man. "I'll try not to keep you long. I understand you're busy."

Stanley Wilson cackled, a rough smoker's laugh. "Appreciate it."

"Tell me about the building evacuation on Friday."

"The weatherman scared everybody shitless. 'Biggest storm in history—'"

Fernandez cut him short. "Someone broke into Mrs. Carlyle's apartment during the storm. Have any ideas?"

"No, sir, sure don't."

"When did you shut the elevators down?"

"Saturday morning. The power went off at ten a.m. Sunday and stayed off two days. On Wednesday I was able to start up the elevators again."

"How did you make out in the storm?"

"I live on the island. I stocked water and put up plywood shutters. The storm knocked down some palms and tore up the grass. No big deal."

"You have access to the Carlyle apartment?"

"Yep. Pass key, and I know their security code."

"When you shut down the elevators, you were the last one to leave the condominium."

"After the DeCiccos, I was last out."

"What time was that?"

"Round about half-past six."

"Did you know the security guard, Leroy Martin?"

"Yep. Nice guy. Leroy was checking things on the property. I was busy. Didn't pay him no mind."

"Any ideas about the robbery?"

"You didn't get this from me, understand?"

Fernandez nodded.

"If I was you, I'd check out that dog walker."

"Why her?"

"That gal has a place in Cancun. I seen pictures."

"Thanks, Stanley." Fernandez glanced at his notes. "You said the last ones to leave were the—"

"Mr. and Mrs. DeCicco. They have the penthouse across the hall." He hesitated before continuing. "I'd tread easy with those people. Vinnie DeCicco is connected."

Shit Fernandez thought. *Mafia. That's all we need.*

* * *

FERNANDEZ HEARD THE BARKING. Barbara McCuskey said she and her husband would keep Bentley in the den while he interviewed the dog walker. Lori Costello was pretty, olive-skinned, willowy and full-breasted, with dark hair and green eyes.

"Let's start with the day the Carlyles left the apartment. When did you come to get the dogs?"

"Around four thirty. It was a confusing situation. I had two dogs from Catamaran II in my car barking like crazy."

"Who was in the apartment at the time?"

"Lisa's people were closing shutters. Mrs. McCuskey was helping her mother pack."

"Anybody else?"

"Not that I could see."

"Did you know Mrs. Carlyle kept expensive jewelry in her bedroom?"

"I'm here every day, and I'm not blind. Sure, I've seen her wearing jewelry."

"Does the dog go into her bedroom?"

"Of course. Bentley is a lap dog, a Cavalier King Charles spaniel. Do you know why King Charles spaniels are linked to English royalty?"

"I have no idea."

"King Charles spaniels were brought into the beds of kings and queens to attract fleas and be bitten instead of the royalty, thereby saving their highnesses from the plague and other diseases."

He glanced at his watch. "Tell me, do you have any idea who may be responsible for the missing jewelry?"

Fernandez noticed her hesitate. In his experience, that was a "tell." She was holding something back.

"C'mon, Lori. Help me. It's important."

She leaned in close. He could smell the fresh-cut lemon scent of her shampoo. Lori whispered, "I can't afford to lose a good customer."

"You have my word."

"That Brad McCuskey is bad news, a gold digger and a letch. He's always hitting on me. And I know he's had affairs with some of my clients."

"Do you want me to talk to him?"

"No. Now I bring my ninety-pound Doberman pinscher on dog walks."

"Good. Glad that problem is solved. Now, please tell me, where were you during Hurricane Irma?"

"At home with my husband in Citrus Manor off Oslo Road. We have a generator, a fenced-in back yard, and I board dogs when clients are away."

"How many dogs during the hurricane?"

"Five including mine."

"Can you make a living doing dog walking?"

She shifted uncomfortably in her chair.

He held up his palms and smiled. "I don't work for the IRS. What you report as income is not my concern, but I have to ask you, Lori; I wouldn't be doing my job if I didn't. Is it true you have a vacation house in Cancun?"

"Yes, it is."

"I didn't know dog walking was so profitable."

"My husband's a lawyer."

* * *

BRAD MCCUSKEY'S GRIN was broad and challenging. Fernandez noticed his cold, appraising eyes.

"Mr. McCuskey, your wife said that she and her mother went to Maitland during the storm. Correct?"

"Yep."

"Why didn't you go with them?"

"I did, and then drove back to Vero. I've been around Florida storms all my life. I wanted to keep an eye on my boat and condo."

"How did you prepare your boat for the storm?"

"I double-tied everything, put on extra bumpers. That's all I could do. Besides, I have insurance."

"Any damage?"

"No. One sailboat in our marina was left with the sail on boom. It got ripped up. That'll probably cost them ten thousand dollars."

"You know a lot about boats?"

"Yeah. Before I went into the SEALs, I was a tester for Evinrude motors. They're built in Wisconsin but tested on Blue Cyprus Lake, twenty miles west of Vero."

"You were a SEAL?"

"Joined in 1980."

"I'm impressed. SEAL Team 6 handled the Osama bin Laden raid in 2011."

"Past my time."

Fernandez asked, "Is there anyone you suspect could be connected to your mother-in-law's robbery?"

"Wilson, the maintenance man. He's always bumming money, and I hear he's got a sick wife and a daughter with drug problems. The guy's sharper than he lets on."

Fernandez leafed through his notebook. "Just a couple more questions. What do you do for a living?"

"A little of this and a little of that."

Fernandez knew from experience that a good interviewer used silence as a weapon. He remained quiet.

McCuskey narrowed his eyes. He wasn't fooled.

"Back to the hurricane," Fernandez said. "When did your power go off?"

"About eight o'clock Saturday night."

"How did you manage?"

"I have a generator."

"Can anyone confirm your whereabouts? Any neighbors interact with you?"

McCuskey looked annoyed. "This is beginning to sound like an interrogation."

"Not at all. I'm curious how an ex-Navy SEAL with the combination to his mother-in-law's apartment spent his time between eight o'clock Saturday night and Monday afternoon. How about telling me?"

Something flickered across McCuskey's face. The ends of his broad mouth turned upwards in the approximation of a smile. "How about fuck you?"

He flipped Fernandez the bird and stormed out.

* * *

"MS. RODRIGUEZ," FRANK BEGAN. "Thanks for being patient."

The cleaning woman's eyes were close-set, her nose beaky and birdlike; she walked with a limp.

"No problem. Mrs. Carlyle is a good customer."

"What time did your crew leave the building Friday?"

"Owners never maintain their shutters proper. It took longer than expected."

Fernandez repeated, "What time did you leave?"

"We finished the shutters and turned the water off. I guess we cleared the building about six o'clock."

"How many in your cleaning crew?"

"Six, plus myself. I recently had a knee replacement, so I wasn't much help."

"You have the combination for this apartment?"

"Yes. Most times no one is home when we clean."

"Your crew was here after the Carlyles left."

"Just so as you know. This crew is like my family—all Puerto Ricans. We clean apartments with valuables in dressers and all kinds of narcotics in bathroom cabinets. I would fire, in a heartbeat, anyone, if I thought they were stealing. My reputation is all I have. I get most new customers from referrals."

"Do you have any idea who could be involved in the robbery?"

"Not my business."

"I'm afraid it is," Fernandez prompted. "Until this robbery is cleared up, your customers may be nervous having your family cleaning their units."

Lisa Rodriguez blanched and hesitated. "I heard Mrs. Carlyle last week on the bedroom phone yelling like crazy at her daughter. She said, 'Any man who marries for money is a leech.'"

"Mrs. Carlyle is old," Fernandez said. "My father's like that. Sometimes old people get confused and say things without thinking."

Lisa Rodriguez shrugged. "Okay. Whatever."

Fernandez didn't press further, suspecting she was withholding information in order not to risk antagonizing Mrs. Carlyle.

After Lisa left, he wandered into the living room and gazed out the window. The beach was deserted. The eastern sky was darkening. Rain was on the way. He smiled, remembering something his brother had said. "Be careful in Florida, Frank. When it rains it pours, and when it shines ... you get melanomas."

* * *

ON HIS WAY OUT OF Ocean Village, Wayne Gibson motioned Fernandez to stop. "Word is Leroy was murdered. Is that right?" the guard asked.

"Looks that way."

"What kind of a fucking world are we living in?"

"When I figure that out, Wayne, I'll let you know. You have my card. Call me if you think of anything."

"Well, I do remember one thing. Leroy Martin was a Navy SEAL, wounded in 'Nam. But he never talked none about the war."

* * *

FERNANDEZ WAS HUNGRY. After he left Ocean Village, he pulled into Archie's half-empty parking lot. The snowbirds were gone. Archie's Seabreeze was a rustic, iconic, rundown Florida beach restaurant across A1A from the ocean. Archie's anchored the bar scene on Hutchinson Island, drawing a mix of gray-bearded bikers, tourists, locals and retirees. In the evening the atmosphere was pure sexual buzz, with a backup of loud, live music. Sunday mornings they held church services—something for everybody.

The waitress sidled up to Fernandez's table, a stocky woman in her mid-fifties, with short gray hair and a *don't-fuck-with-me* attitude. Janice had a gift for schmoozing with the serious drinkers while placating the rowdies.

"Frank. Long time no see."

"Hey, Janice."

"What's doing with the wife thing?"

"We're giving it another shot."

"Sorry to hear it. What're you having?"

"Hamburger medium, a Guinness, and homemade key lime pie."

Janice leaned in close. "I heard you got some lead rattling around in your chest that the surgeons can't remove. Is that true?"

Fernandez took a deep breath. "Right."

She dropped her voice. "Life can be shit sometimes. I'm here for you, my friend, and I'm not going anywhere." Janice gave him a fist bump, and then she headed for the kitchen.

When the Guinness came, Fernandez took a long, slow swallow. His phone chirped. He saw it was his wife.

"Hi, honey," Maris said. "I'm sorry. We can't make it this weekend. Charlie has a doctor's appointment, and the museum is mounting a Salvador Dali-Pablo Picasso retrospective. I need to be here to help out. The first time the two Spanish painters—"

Fernandez interrupted, "What kind of appointment?"

"Charlie doesn't talk much, although he understands what I'm saying, and he loves drawing with crayons. He might become an artist. You know, Pablo Picasso's first word was '*piz*,' short for *lapis*, Spanish for 'pencil.'"

"Let me speak to the little genius."

"Now's not a good time. Where are you, Frank?" Maris said, changing the subject. "I hear background noises."

"Archie's. And Janice is looking hotter than ever."

"The waitress? I thought she was in a nursing home."

"Right. And Medicare is picking up my bar tab. Let's talk later."

* * *

"WANT COMPANY?"

The man standing by Fernandez's table was dark-haired and had a furtive twinkle in his eyes. Fernandez had to admit that Ben Herman, for all his obnoxious ways and superior manner, was a newspaperman who pursued stories with grim determination and integrity. Fernandez also thought he was a pain in the ass.

"Hello, Ben."

Fernandez closed his notebook and shook hands.

Ben Herman signaled Janice. "Dewars on the rocks."

He squeezed into the booth opposite Fernandez. "Working a case?"

"No comment."

"I'm just doing my thing and living the dream. But we all like to eat, right?"

Herman gulped his scotch. "I have a freelance deal with the *Palm Beach Post*. They pay me for each piece that's accepted." The newsman caught Janice's attention. He raised his empty glass.

"Have you met the new police chief?" Herman asked.

"Yeah."

"And?"

"Too early to tell. Beauvoir looks competent. She's under pressure being Fort Pierce's first Haitian female police chief."

"You working the Pepper Beach murder?"

"No. I'm doing Lou Brumberg a favor. One of his neighbors had a break-in during the hurricane. I'm checking it out."

"Fort Pierce has one of the highest violent crime rates in Florida and you're investigating break-ins? You're fucking with me, Frank."

"I'm not a kid anymore. I've got health issues and a wife and son to think about. My wife wants me to give up my investigating business, but I'm not quite ready to put on a paper hat and serve hamburgers at McDonald's."

Fernandez emptied his beer. "You've been around, Ben. Maybe you can help. Something doesn't add up. I just can't put my finger on it."

"I'm listening."

"The robbery case I'm working occurred during Hurricane Irma. The thieves took jewelry worth over seventy-eight thousand dollars; they also made off with an inexpensive piece of art, a Picasso print. It doesn't add up, because the place was filled with really valuable artwork."

Herman scoffed. "Not everybody's an art history major. They probably thought the reproduction was an original painting."

Fernandez shook his head. "The thieves carried waterproof plastic for a heist in a Category Five storm. The plastic wasn't for the jewelry—gold doesn't tarnish."

"I was an investigative reporter for twenty years," Herman said. "Somebody's tossing you a red herring."

...6

IT WAS AFTER SEVEN O'CLOCK when Fernandez arrived back at his apartment. Dinner was leftover barbecue chicken nuked in the microwave.

He wanted to keep moving on the case, hoping movement would spark progress. An investigator's holy trinity was motive, means and opportunity. "And as for motives," an FBI instructor had once told him, "look for *at least* one of the four L's: *Love, Lust, Lucre* and *Loathing*."

Sitting at his desk, Fernandez started a timeline:

Friday, September 8th—Residents evacuated building
Saturday, September 9th—Bridges to Island closed
Sunday, September 10th—Hurricane Irma hit Ft. Pierce
Monday, September 11th—Security guards returned
Wednesday, September 13th—Mrs. Carlyle returned

	Suspects:	
Cleaners	Lisa Rodriguez	Left 6:00
Maintenance Man	Stanley Wilson	Left 6:30
Security guard	Leroy Martin	Left 5:30
Neighbors	DeCiccos	Left 5:45
Son-in-law	Brad McCuskey	Left 5:30

Fernandez omitted from his list Lori Costello, the dog walker, and Grace Carlyle and her daughter, Barbara. He felt there was a low probability of their complicity in the robbery, based on what he knew and felt.

When his phone rang, it was Maris.

"I'm sorry about this weekend, Frank."

"It's just as well. I'm tied up."

"You mentioned a stolen painting?"

"It's a confusing case, Maris. During the hurricane there was a robbery in a condo in Ocean Village. When the owner returned after the storm, she discovered valuable jewelry missing, along with a reproduction of a Picasso painting. The odd thing is, there was valuable original art hanging in plain sight that wasn't touched."

"Maybe the burglars assumed it was valuable. Today the Chinese are mass-producing reproductions that take an expert to differentiate from originals."

"You could be right."

"Which Picasso was it?"

"*Boy with a Pipe.*"

"I believe it was exhibited some years ago at the Riverside Art Museum. Unfortunately, I never got to see it."

Maris was quiet for a moment. "As I remember, that painting sold at auction at Sotheby's for a record amount of money. You might find it informative to talk to the Riverside Museum's director, Justin Williams. Justin was helpful to me when I managed the gallery in Fort Pierce. If you call him, use my name."

His phone flashed.

"Another call. I've got to go. Give Charlie a hug. Love you, bye."

* * *

"NEED YOUR HELP," Lou Brumberg said.

"Another robbery in your building?"

"No." The ex–police chief exhaled loudly. "When we returned from 'Nam, people treated us like shit; no welcome home parties. Some guys even got spit on. It's not right that Vietnam vets were ignored."

"Where are you going with this, Lou?"

"That fellow killed on Pepper Beach was an ex-Navy SEAL. He was wounded bad ... in Vietnam."

"Yeah. I heard that."

"Here's the deal. I talked to some guys at our SEAL Museum. Bottom line, we put together a pot to investigate Leroy Martin's murder."

"That's Garcella Beauvoir's job."

"I don't reckon that lady's got her feet wet yet," Brumberg said. "Listen up, Frank. There's an unspoken code in the SEALs. We never left a teammate behind—dead or alive. Somebody murdered Leroy, and you need to find who killed him."

Silence.

"Talk to your wife, Frank. Her old man was a SEAL. Charlie never made it back from 'Nam. Tell Maris you're too busy to help find the killer of a fellow SEAL. That girl will set you straight in a heartbeat."

"We might have a problem, Lou," Fernandez said quietly. "I'll give you a heads-up. Leroy Martin might have been involved in the Carlyle heist."

"Great God in heaven," Brumberg sputtered. "Now you're going to spit on the poor bastard's grave."

* * *

FERNANDEZ ADMIRED THE UNSPOKEN CODE of Navy SEALS. It was an obligation made to the living that remained in death.

Once, he'd believed the FBI held similar values. But, after he'd nearly died in a botched drug bust, Fernandez learned it was an FBI informer who had alerted the drug traffickers. When he returned to duty after three months of recuperation, Fernandez had confronted the man who had leaked—his boss, William Glenner.

Glenner had said, "Leaking is a varsity sport in Washington, necessary to satisfy the gods of political expediency. By protecting the drug traffickers, the FBI was able to neutralize the Cali and Escobar cartels."

He'd said that in his job, he needed to do what he needed to do so the Bureau could get funding for guys like Fernandez to do what they needed to do.

Fernandez poured two fingers of single malt and anchored himself in his recliner. He dozed off.

In a recurring dream he found himself back in that dingy Miami warehouse with two sniper bullets ricocheting around his chest; the excruciating pain; every breath a knife turning in his chest.

He saw the pulsing red blood before he collapsed to the warehouse floor. Then the blackness mercifully came, swimming up and over him in waves.

...7

SATURDAY MORNING Fernandez snapped awake, sweat dampening his face. He unconsciously rubbed the pink scars on his chest where bullet fragments still remained—too near the heart to extract. The apartment was quiet. He decided to visit the Fort Pierce Saturday Market to pick up tomatoes and talk to Willie Youngblood, the Highwayman artist. A soft, humid breeze ruffled the tops of the palm trees.

The Farmers' Market was busy. Every week the tents were set up in the same spots: kettle corn at one end, fresh farm products at the other. Flower vendors favored locations across from the library. The coffee and bakery vendors chose to be near the water.

Fernandez crossed Indian River Drive and entered the craft market area, bordered by a white picket fence. Five rows of vendors under canvas tents displayed their wares. September was off-season; nonetheless, a small crowd milled around, many with dogs on leashes.

As he passed the local writers' booth, Fernandez noticed his neighbor, Avram Markus, deep in conversation with one of the authors: a short, elderly man with a gray goatee. Both men were speaking fluent German. He didn't intrude on their conversation. Instead he spotted Youngblood standing by his Highwaymen artwork.

Willie Youngblood was a professional painter and amateur arsonist. Fernandez had cleared Youngblood a few years earlier of charges related to the fire that had destroyed the art museum his wife, Maris, had been managing.

Fernandez knew Willie had his ears to the ground. Fort Pierce was a small town. Youngblood had a high I.Q. but adopted a folksy, old black Highwayman mannerism because it helped sell paintings.

"Hello, Cap'n. How's it going?"

"Good, Willie. How about you?"

"I'm walkin' on my heels," Youngblood cackled, "to save my soul."

"I'm investigating a robbery that occurred during the storm. Know anything about it?"

Youngblood looked up with a tired smile. "Can't say as I do, Cap'n."

"The thieves stole jewelry and a fake Pablo Picasso painting."

"That Picasso muthafucka stole his stuff from African artists."

"Come on, Willie, the guy was a genius. Everybody knows that."

Avram Markus materialized at Fernandez's shoulder. "The gentleman is correct. Picasso's interest in African art has been well documented. Picasso's *Demoiselles D'Avignon* depicts five naked women, a couple with African masks for faces."

Youngblood whipped out his iPhone and tapped. "Here, take a gander. Them's bare-ass African girls, not mademoiselles from Armentières."

Fernandez tried to hide his impatience. "I'm not here for an art lesson. I'm investigating a robbery."

Willie shook his head. "Wish I could help you, Cap'n."

Avram Markus spoke a quiet aside to Youngblood. Fernandez couldn't hear what they were saying. He saw Markus select two paintings and hand over money.

Youngblood pocketed the bills and rejoined Fernandez. In a low voice he whispered, "Cap'n, word is they be pullin' up *more* than fish off Fisherman's Wharf."

"You mean jewelry?"

Youngblood shrugged, and then he turned to help a potential buyer.

Fernandez called the police station. He asked for the police captain.

"Beauvoir here."

"This is Fernandez. Get people to Fisherman's Wharf. I think we found the Carlyle jewelry."

Within minutes Fernandez heard the sounds of police cruisers heading north on U.S. Route 1. Blue strobe lights were whirling and sirens were whooping.

*   *   *

FISHERMAN'S WHARF WAS LOCATED at the foot of the South Causeway Bridge. Curious onlookers watched from behind the yellow and black CRIME SCENE DO NOT CROSS tape that the police had stretched across the parking lot. Two men were seated in the back of a patrol car. The breeze was light and cool off the Indian River.

A uniform stopped Fernandez at the tape. Chief Beauvoir motioned him through. "Thanks for the tip. Should I ask where you got it?"

"A source."

She gave him a hard look but didn't press the issue. "Those guys in the car were bottom-fishing. Around six a.m., the skinny one snagged a gold necklace, and word spread. An hour ago, his buddy pulled in a man's Rolex watch. I expect there's more to be found."

"How are you handling the recovery operation?"

"The boat repair yard next door has contract salvers. They'll check the river bottom with scanning equipment. I don't want to waste time on beer cans and iron scrap. If they get a positive reading, I'll send police divers down.

Small items like rings and earrings may be hard to find in shifting sand. But it's all insured, correct?"

"Yes."

"Then your job is over."

"Not exactly. We have a situation. The Pepper Beach murder victim, Leroy Martin, was a Navy SEAL. The guys at the SEAL Museum took up a collection—"

"And they hired you," she broke in, "to interfere in an investigation, which I offered you a role in, but you refused to get involved, right?"

Fernandez fumbled for words. "I can't say why I got drawn in. It has to do with the SEALs' unspoken code: 'No one left behind.'" He cleared his throat. "As old-fashioned as it may sound, I find honor a commodity in very limited supply these days."

Garcella Beauvoir gave him a brief smile, but there was a hint of steel in her voice. "Keep me informed of everything you find. Not crumbs, everything."

"Agreed."

Fernandez felt a twinge of excitement. It was good to be back in the game. Grace Carlyle's jewelry had been recovered. He puzzled over Ben Herman's warning: The jewelry heist was a red herring.

PART II

A RED HERRING

"A red herring misleads or distracts from an important issue."
—*Wikipedia*

...8

SATURDAY AFTERNOON FERNANDEZ drove to Vero Beach to interview the executive director of the Riverside Art Museum. In the lobby was a bronze plaque.

> Riverside Art Museum, established 1985 as a center for fine arts. In 2007 the Peter Cushing Memorial Sculpture Garden was added, followed in 2011 by the Grace and Anthony Carlyle Exhibition Wing.

"Mr. Fernandez?" said a short, gray-haired woman with a soft voice and a tight smile. "I'm Margaret Adkins, Mr. Williams' administrative assistant. The director will see you now."

Justin Williams' office was equipped with a dark mahogany executive desk, a sofa and coffee table resting on plush Persian carpet. The back wall was a huge pane of glass looking out on the Indian River.

Williams was a tall, distinguished-looking man in his mid-seventies. His silver hair was brushed back from a narrow forehead. A red linen handkerchief showed above the pocket of a navy sport coat.

The director clasped his hands on his desk, waiting for Fernandez to begin.

"Thank you for seeing me on such short notice, sir."

"Please don't call me 'sir.' It makes me feel old," Williams said. "And how is your charming wife?"

"Maris is winding up her job at the Dali Museum."

"The Dali is mounting a Picasso-Dali show." Williams shook his head. "People pay tribute to their idols, not wishing to witness their feet of clay."

"Sorry. I don't follow you."

"Dali and Picasso were creative geniuses—no doubt. The two Spaniards were also flawed individuals. Salvador Dali sympathized with Hitler, and as for Picasso, the man was a bloody Communist."

Fernandez nodded absently and took out his notebook. "I'm investigating a crime that took place during Hurricane Irma. Perhaps you've heard that one of your museum patrons, Mrs. Grace Carlyle's apartment was broken into during the storm."

"I know Grace. Dear woman must be terribly upset."

"Other than jewelry," Fernandez said, "the other missing item was an uninsured Picasso print." He swiped through the photos on his phone screen until he came to the shot of the missing painting Barbara McCuskey had forwarded.

"Ah. *Boy with a Pipe*," Williams said.

Fernandez peered at his iPhone picture. The lad in the painting was dressed in overalls, holding a pipe in his left hand. On his head was a garland of what looked like roses, and painted on the wall behind him were circular arrangements of flowers.

"The general consensus among art critics, myself included," Williams said, "is that *Garçon à la Pipe* is not one of Picasso's masterpieces. In my opinion, the portrait is a delightful work of visual art."

Williams narrowed his eyes. "And how is your investigation of Mrs. Carlyle's unfortunate event progressing?"

"This morning, portions of her jewelry were recovered from the Indian River. Depending on water currents, shifting sands and luck, we might recover it all. It's my guess that the break-in had nothing to do with the jewelry; the artwork must have been the target. Maris felt you could help with my investigation."

Williams sat for a moment in thoughtful silence. "At the time of the sale, museum directors were shocked that a pleasant, minor Picasso painting could command such a price. It demonstrated how the marketplace had become divorced from true values of art.

"We no longer know what a painting is worth. Prices are driven up in the rarified strata of the hyper rich. You might not be able to put a price on beauty, but you can put a price on a name. And Picasso had a name."

"Who purchased the Picasso painting?"

"As I recall, it was an unidentified bidder, rumored to be a Russian oligarch. Someday we may learn the real identity of the buyer, though in the secretive world of art collection, that is not a certainty."

"How much did the painting sell for?"

"Hard to keep track. I don't remember."

"My wife said the Picasso was on exhibit here some years ago."

"True. *Boy with a Pipe* was given on loan to our museum for a Picasso retrospective in 2002. That was before my time here."

"Could anyone have tampered with the painting at the museum?"

The director frowned. "Highly unlikely. Valuable artwork on loan is protected in shipment and under twenty-four-hour guard during an exhibit. The insurance companies establish the guidelines."

"Is it conceivable the painting in the Carlyle apartment was the original Picasso and not a reproduction?"

"No, and let me tell you why. When the painting went on auction, it was authenticated by Sotheby's and, I'm certain, by the buyer."

Fernandez noticed Justin Williams' eyes flicker. He was lying.

"Thank you for your time," he said. "I have one more question. You said you know Mrs. Carlyle?"

"Of course. If you noticed the plaque in our lobby, both of Grace's husbands were generous donors. When I took over in 2010, new funding was a priority." Williams sighed deeply. "Unfortunately, money is the mother's milk of art museums, as it is for politics. Pragmatism rules, I'm afraid."

"Pragmatism?"

"Grace's second husband, Anthony Carlyle, was a benefactor. He gave the museum funding and donated some of his wife's collection. I put up with him."

"You don't sound like you cared for the man."

"Since you're Maris's husband, I'll speak frankly. Anthony Carlyle was as deceitful a man as I've ever met. He married Grace for her money. In my book, the man was a total shit. When he died in the boat mishap, I couldn't have been more pleased."

Justin Williams stood up. "Is there anything else I could help you with?"

...9

"WHEN HE DIED IN THE BOAT MISHAP." Justin Williams' words echoed in Fernandez's brain as he drove south on U.S. 1. It was a surprise to learn about the death of Grace Carlyle's husband, Anthony Carlyle.

Fernandez realized his interview with the museum director had been slipshod. He had allowed himself to be distracted, and as a result, he'd neglected to bring up the Leroy Martin murder case. Williams had controlled the meeting.

He pulled into the McDonald's drive-thru off Oslo Road, ordered a black coffee, and parked. Fernandez deliberated a moment and then telephoned Williams' assistant, requesting Leroy Martin's employment records and next of kin information be faxed to his office.

Margaret Adkins said she would check with the art museum director.

Back on the highway, he passed a liquor store. Avram Markus came to mind. The old man reminded him of his father. He parked, went in and purchased a bottle of Metaxa 7 Star Greek brandy. The gift would give him another opportunity to spend time with his new neighbor.

His cell phone chirped.

"Fernandez?" Garcella Beauvoir said. "Just got word. Leroy Martin's mobile home was torched. All that's left are ashes, a burnt-out trailer, and the stink of kerosene. You might want to have a look."

* * *

THE FIRE WAS OUT by the time Fernandez arrived on the scene, just off Indrio Road. He saw a soot-blackened trailer in the midst of a clearing, surrounded by a patch of scraggly hardwood and pine. The acrid odor of fire and ash hung in the air.

Fernandez found the fireman in charge, a short, squat, powerful-looking man who seemed to be perspiring heavily. A walkie-talkie hitched to his belt squawked unceasingly.

"I'm working the case," Fernandez said. "Who reported the fire?"

"A motorcyclist riding by saw a flash and called nine-one-one. If the ground hadn't been soaked from the hurricane, this whole area would be a tinderbox."

"Arson?"

"You can still smell the kerosene if you get close."

"Any tire marks?"

"With the rain, the access road is all mud. If there were tracks, our trucks probably ruined them. Sorry."

"Anything I can work with?"

The fireman winked. "Sometimes fine citizens grab the trailer insurance, sell the lot … take a trip to Las Vegas or wherever. Wouldn't be the first time."

Fernandez took a final look at the charred wreckage. Leroy Martin wasn't going to Vegas. The ex-Navy SEAL was destined for a cemetery.

*   *   *

THE WESTERN SKY PURPLED as Fernandez drove to his office at 505 South 2nd Street in Fort Pierce. After leaving the FBI, Fernandez had analyzed areas in Florida with the highest crime rates. At the time, crime in Fort

Pierce was on the rise. Believing the market for security services would rise proportionately, Fernandez had purchased the assets of a small security agency.

However, Fort Pierce residents were different than their neighbors in Vero Beach to the north or Stuart to the south. The folk living west of Federal Highway in Fort Pierce didn't require professional security services. They purchased Dobermans and Smith and Wessons. Under Florida's Stand Your Ground law, anyone could invoke self-defense if he or she felt threatened.

To the east on North and South Hutchinson Island, senior citizens frequented early bird restaurants and didn't stray from their gated communities at night.

Fernandez's office felt hot and stuffy. He flipped on the ceiling fan switch and listened to it creak metallically as it beat the air and stirred the dust.

A fax from Margaret Adkins was waiting for him. He studied the brief report.

Personnel File: Leroy Martin
Employee Performance Review: January 12, 2017
Address: 17 St. Carlos Lane, Fort Pierce, Florida 34951
Telephone: 772-467-0800
Email: Leroym@aol.com
Contact information—Sister: Becky Foster, 410-675-9922
Leroy Martin was hired March 17, 2001. He has continued to successfully perform his duties as a security guard. There have been no disciplinary action reports, nor complaints from fellow museum workers or visitors. A recognition letter was presented to acknowledge his loyalty and commitment to the museum.
Scheduled retirement: January 2018.

Fernandez telephoned Leroy Martin's sister. She picked up on the second ring.

"Is this Becky Foster?"

A guarded voice replied. "Yes?"

"Ms. Foster, I'm working with the Fort Pierce police investigating your brother's … tragic death."

"Roy was a special person." He heard an intake of breath. "My brother led a star-crossed life. When he graduated Annapolis High, Leroy received a scholarship to study in New York City. If it wasn't for Vietnam, my brother could have made a career out of art."

Fernandez remained quiet. He understood the sister's need to unload feelings.

Becky Foster sighed again. "I begged Roy to take a college deferment, but he was stubborn. He wanted to serve in the Navy. He told me he would go back to school when he returned."

Fernandez heard quiet sobbing. "It wasn't to be. He came home in 1967. Instead of art school, Roy went to Walter Reed Army Medical Center in Washington, D.C."

"I understand," Fernandez said.

"How can anyone possibly understand?" she snapped.

"I was also injured in the line of duty. The bullet fragments inside my chest are too close to my heart to operate."

"I'm sorry."

"If you will allow me, ma'am, I would like to ask some questions that may help find your brother's killer."

"Go ahead."

"Besides you, did Leroy have any family?"

"An ex-wife and daughter in California. After my brother recovered from his surgeries and was discharged, he joined the Baltimore Police Department.

"It was in 1968—the year of the riots. Roy worked long hours under stressful conditions. Like a lot of cops, he tried to manage the pressure with alcohol. His wife, who was no great shakes to begin with, filed for divorce, took their daughter Edie, and moved to Los Angeles."

Fernandez listened, taking notes.

"Roy said the winter weather in Baltimore made his face wounds ache. He moved to Florida and found a job as a museum security guard."

"I noticed in his personnel file he was planning to retire this year. Did he discuss post-retirement plans?"

Becky Foster sounded pensive. "Roy was going to Los Angeles. He wanted to rebuild a relationship with his daughter, to help her get on her feet. Edie can't hold a job. She's in drug rehab somewhere."

"Los Angeles is an expensive town," Fernandez said. "How was your brother fixed financially?"

"I never asked."

"Please call me if you think of anything else," he said.

"It might help if I had your name and number."

After disconnecting, Fernandez felt fatigued. His blood sugar level was cratering. He searched in his desk for M&M's. Then Fernandez remembered the bottle of Metaxa in his car. *Candy is dandy. But liquor is quicker.*

...10

"I WANTED TO REPAY your hospitality," Fernandez said, "and replenish your brandy inventory."

"Nonsense," his neighbor answered, waving a hand dismissively. "Come in. Come in."

Markus uncapped the Metaxa. "Our building manager told me you were involved with the investigation of the man murdered in this apartment."

"Involved, but not by choice." Fernandez related the events surrounding Earle Mayfield's death. "Colonel Mayfield had served in the Korean War as a battalion commander. In 1950 the Army integrated its troops, and black and white soldiers fought alongside one another. Some white officers retained racist feelings. Mayfield was a prime example. He unfairly caused an African American war hero, Captain Ben Walker, to be dishonorably discharged and imprisoned."

Markus's eyebrows rose as he handed Fernandez a snifter of brandy.

"Mayfield was also responsible for the mass execution of hundreds of innocent South Korean refugees. One eyewitness survivor of the Pukhan River Massacre was a young girl who came to live in the United States, Fort Pierce in fact. She now owns the Seoul Garden Restaurant near Virginia Avenue.

"I was convinced Myung Kym or her grandson Ji-hoon Kym had murdered Mayfield in revenge. And for good reason." Fernandez downed his drink. "I was wrong. But Ben Walker eventually received his Medal of Honor in a White House ceremony."

Markus picked up his cane. "Nature calls."

Fernandez noticed Willie Youngblood's paintings stacked in a corner. On the wall was a painting of a woman and child and a fiddler.

When Markus returned, Fernandez said, "Interesting painting. Who was the artist?"

"Marc Chagall."

"May I ask why you chose this painting?"

Silence fell between them.

The old man's voice trailed off as he gazed at the painting of the fiddler and the mother and child. "The fiddler in the small villages in Russia played at births, weddings and

... deaths. Chagall is telling us that life is a balancing act; a precarious journey filled with challenges."

Fernandez thought his neighbor had crossed the line into drunkenness. "Life is unfair," Markus muttered. "Why should death be any different?"

Avram Markus poured himself another brandy. "Cherish your family, my dear Mr. Fernandez. I speak from sad experience. In the end, family is all we have. You'll do well to remember that. And *never* forget to tell them you love them."

* * *

IT WAS LATE WHEN FERNANDEZ returned to his apartment. Consuming brandy on an empty stomach had made him lightheaded. He recalled Markus's words: "Never forget to tell your family you love them."

Without considering how late it was, he tapped in Maris' number.

"Hello," a sleepy, anxious voice answered. "What's wrong?"

"Nothing's wrong. I wanted to tell you I love you."

"At this ungodly hour, you wake me up to tell me you love me." She exhaled loudly. "You had sex with that white trash waitress tramp and you're feeling guilty. That's it, isn't it?"

"No, honey. I had a little brandy with a neighbor and ... Maris? Maris?" he echoed into the dead phone.

...11

SUNDAY MORNING FERNANDEZ AWOKE after a night of broken sleep. He was tired, frustrated and edgy. When his phone rang, he hoped it was Maris. Instead it was his brother, Martin.

"It's Dad," Martin said in an agitated voice. "I got a call from North Oaks last night. Dad wheeled himself through the front entrance shouting to passing motorists, 'Help! Help! Save me! I'm a Korean veteran. They're holding me prisoner.'"

"Jesus," Fernandez mumbled.

"It took three nurses to subdue him. They had to transfer him into the Memory Care unit." Fernandez heard his brother cough nervously. "Dad doesn't recognize me anymore. He keeps calling me Frank."

"Should I come to Baltimore?"

"No. They're giving him a cocktail of antidepressants. It will take a while to see how his mind and body react." Martin heaved another sigh. "You wouldn't recognize our old man, Frank. When he's out of the wheelchair, he walks with a living-dead shuffle."

After hanging up, Fernandez sat for a long time, staring at a framed photograph of his father. It spoke to him from a distant past. Once he and his father had been close. All that had changed when he'd decided to join the FBI.

His father had preached to Fernandez and his brother that as a minority, they needed a profession. He distrusted politicians. "With a profession," his father counseled, "if you're persecuted, you can pick up and move and take your profession with you."

Fernandez called Maris to tell her his father had dementia. He knew his wife was fond of Luis Fernandez, fonder at times than she was of his son.

"I'm sorry you have to go through this, Frank," Maris commiserated. "Be grateful your father came back from a war. Luis lived a long life. I wish I could have said the same for my dad."

"When this case is over, honey," Fernandez said, "I'll find a place on North Hutchinson for the three of us, and … sign the teaching contract."

"Did you talk to Justin Williams at the museum?"

"He wasn't all that helpful."

"I checked," Maris said. "Picasso's *Boy with a Pipe* was auctioned for over a hundred million dollars in 2004."

When Fernandez didn't respond, she added, "Listen to me, Frank. If there's a multi-million-dollar Picasso floating around and one man has been murdered already, then I don't want you messing with this case. Let the FBI handle it, not you. That is, if you ever want Charlie and me back in Fort Pierce. You know I'm serious."

PART III

THE ART CRIME INVESTIGATOR

Quis custodiet ipsos custodes?

Who shall guard the guards?

...12

VIRGINIA BAKER WAS AN FBI computer analyst with a prodigious memory. For years, when he lived in Washington, Fernandez and Virginia Baker had had an on-and-off relationship of convenience between two agents grounded on sexual, not emotional needs. Their liaisons were sporadic, usually weeks or months apart. Fernandez had been content to let Virginia initiate them.

Fernandez called Virginia Baker at home.

"A voice from my sordid past," she said. "Hello, Frank. I don't suppose you're calling for phone sex."

"Not this time, Virginia."

"How did you make out with the lead therapy?"

"I'm still here."

"Tell me, Frank, does your chest still rattle when you have an orgasm?"

"I'll have my wife call and discuss it with you."

"No thanks, I'll pass. What can I do for you?"

"I need some information, Virginia."

Her tone changed. "I'm planning early retirement, Frank. It's got to the point where I hate going to work every day; no sense of purpose anymore. The Bureau's become a fucking bureaucracy. You need to protect your turf, your ass and your career. Nobody has your back anymore."

"Been there, done that."

"Yeah," Virginia groused. "I remember the Miami warehouse *incident*."

"I forgot about that remarkable memory of yours."

"No you didn't, Frank. That's why you called."

"Does the Bureau investigate art thefts?"

"We did for a while. A Rapid Deployment Art Crime Team was set up after you left. They recovered millions in lost artwork. When the new administration came in, the program was shut down. Agents were diverted to rounding up *illegals*."

"Who was in charge of the Art Crime squad?"

"Quint Langstaff. Good man, as I recall. When his group was disbanded, Langstaff retired and started his own firm."

"Do you know how I could reach the guy?"

"I have a good memory, but not that good. Google him. And, by the way, Frank, how's your frumpy waitress friend from the biker bar?"

"Janice? How the hell do you know Janice?"

"Your tax dollars at work, sweetheart. *Ciao*."

* * *

FERNANDEZ OPENED A SEARCH ENGINE. He typed in *Quint Langstaff, art security* and received a cluster of hits. Fernandez learned Langstaff was a fifty-nine-year-old former senior investigator for the FBI's Art Crime Team. The man had a long and distinguished career: many successful cases, multiple medals and awards.

It was three p.m. when Fernandez placed the call.

"Langstaff," a gruff voice answered.

"My name is Frank Fernandez. I was—"

"*The* Saint Fernandez?"

Fernandez paused, drew a breath. "That was twenty-five years ago."

"You're a legend, man. You spoke truth to power, and the Bureau got spanked by Attorney General Reno for the Waco fuck-up. So tell me, to what do I owe this honor?"

"I heard you retired."

"I was nudged out. The new administration shut us down and disbanded my rapid deployment Art Crime Team. Their voter base wasn't focused on art crime—it was considered victimless. The Bureau's resources were shifted to immigration and terrorism.

"Those areas are important, I'll grant you," Langstaff grunted, "but downplaying art crime was shortsighted. During my stint, we recovered more than three hundred million dollars' worth of stolen artwork and rare historic masterpieces."

Fernandez cleared his throat. "I'm working as a private investigator on a robbery case. During Hurricane Irma, valuable jewelry was stolen from an upscale Hutchinson Island apartment, along with a copy of a Picasso painting. A few days ago, we located the missing jewelry—dumped in the local river."

"Good. So what's the problem?"

"Why would somebody go to the trouble, in the midst of a major storm, to steal a fake piece of art?"

"Maybe they didn't know it was fake."

"Trust me—they knew."

"You said the item in question was a Picasso? Which one?"

"*Boy with a Pipe*."

Langstaff whistled. "No shit? That baby's worth over a hundred mil. Where are you located, Frank?"

"Fort Pierce."

"That's not too far away. I live in the Villages, near Orlando—a Disney World for adults. We have the most golf courses of any senior community in the country."

"Sounds nice."

"Also the highest genital herpes rate."

"Seniors?"

"Viagra."

"So there's rampant sex at the Villages?"

"Don't I wish." Langstaff chuckled. "Unfortunately for me, my girlfriend has a concealed weapon permit for her .38 Special, and she scores 200 out of 220 on the range. If you remember, that's in the expert category."

"Smart woman."

"How about I drive down in the morning?"

"Sounds good. What's your fee?"

"For Saint Fernandez, it's on the house. You buy lunch."

After giving directions, he telephoned Garcella Beauvoir. Fernandez outlined Quint Langstaff's credentials. She agreed to meet at eleven a.m.

Fernandez checked his watch: 3:45. The football game between the Miami Dolphins and the Los Angeles Chargers had been delayed because of the weather. He decided to prepare for Langstaff's visit. On a legal pad, Fernandez listed the facts as he knew them.

Fri. 08 Sept—Grace Carlyle left apt. 5 p.m.
Barbara McCuskey left with mother
Brad McCuskey left 5:30
Lori Costello (dog walker) left 4:30
Leroy Martin (guard) left 5:30
Lisa Rodriguez (cleaners) left 6 p.m.
DeCiccos (neighbors) left 5:45

Stanley Wilson (maintenance man) left 6:30
Sat. 09 Sept—Bridges to Hutchinson Island closed
Power shut off 10 a.m. (No elevators)
Sat. Sun. 09-10—Hurricane Irma hit Ft. Pierce
Sun. 10 Sept—Leroy Martin murdered
Wed. 13 Sept— Power on in a.m.
Grace Carlyle returns to apt.
Sat. 16 Sept—Jewelry recovered at Fisherman's Wharf

Fernandez flipped on the television. He got a beer and sipped it slowly, watching the Dolphins beat the Chargers in the final minutes of the storm-delayed opener. Cody Parker, a young second team kicker, connected on a 54-yard field goal with 65 seconds remaining.

"Wow. Parker's last-minute kick was a heart-stopper," the announcer crowed. "But better late than never, right?"

Fernandez gazed at his father's photograph. He tried to put out of his mind Martin's comment: "Dad walks with a living-dead shuffle." He was glad his father and he had reconciled after so many years. Fernandez raised his glass in a toast.

"Here's to us, Dad. Better late than never, right?" A tear crept into his eye. He feared it was to be *never*.

...13

QUINT LANGSTAFF WAS A DOUR, weary-looking man. Deep furrows lined his broad, suntanned face. He was beginning to go bald. The former head of the FBI Art Crime Team was wearing jeans, a black polo shirt, and a crumpled gray jacket.

Garcella Beauvoir stood up, trying to be polite, and shook hands. "Thanks for coming."

The man opened his palms. "Anything for Saint Fernandez."

Beauvoir exchanged a puzzled look with Fernandez. "Saint who?"

"This guy was a legend in the FBI."

"So was J. Edgar," Fernandez broke in. "If we're finished reminiscing, let's get to work." He reviewed the Carlyle robbery: the recovered jewelry, the missing artwork, and the murder of Leroy Martin. Fernandez repeated his belief that stealing the replicated Picasso portrait was the primary motive for the break-in.

"It's not surprising," Langstaff said. "Art crimes are reaching epic proportions."

"Epic?" Garcella snorted. "Isn't that an exaggeration?"

"According to Interpol, art crimes were exceeded only by drug trafficking, money laundering and arms dealing. Estimates put the losses at four to six billion dollars worldwide."

Beauvoir's eyes widened. She opened her desk drawer and removed a wire-bound note pad. Fernandez also started taking notes.

"Museum heists grab the most headlines," Langstaff said, "but they represent only a tenth of art crimes. Fifty-two percent of pilfered artworks are taken from private homes, ten percent from galleries, and eight percent from churches."

"I grew up in Boston," Garcella said. "I heard about the Isabella Stewart Gardner Museum robbery."

"That heist was thirty years ago," Langstaff said. "It's still unsolved. The take was close to five hundred million dollars. The Gardner robbery was a wakeup call to art museums. As a result, they're installing ultrasonic sensors to keep track of activity in a gallery, but it's unlikely art theft will end.

"Recently an armed trio of thieves pulled off a heist in Sweden. The gang entered the National Museum in Stockholm just before closing, threatened staff with submachine guns, and then ripped a Rembrandt and two Renoirs from the walls. The thieves escaped in a boat moored near the museum. The stolen paintings, estimated to be worth thirty million dollars, have yet to be found.

"If I were on the Stockholm Museum case," Langstaff continued, "I would start by checking the museum's staff. People think museums are secure guardians of valuable artwork, but the fact is, ninety percent of museum thefts are inside jobs."

"Insiders?" Garcella Beauvoir said, looking doubtful.

"Believe me, insiders know how to exploit museum vulnerabilities: a ticket taker, a docent, an outside contractor, a guide, a security guard, an executive, even a trustee or wealthy patron—anyone tempted to use his or her access to walk away with a piece of art worth millions."

"Didn't an employee steal the *Mona Lisa*?" she asked.

"True. One of the biggest art crimes in history was an inside job. In 1911, the *Mona Lisa* disappeared from the Louvre. French detectives interviewed every member of the museum staff and all contractors, including an Italian glazier named Vincenzo Peruggia. The glazier should have been a prime suspect. He had means, motive, and opportunity and was one of the craftsmen who had constructed the wood and glass box that housed Leonardo's masterpiece.

"Peruggia knew the *Mona Lisa* was secured to the wall by only four metal hooks and guarded by an old military pensioner. One fine summer day the glazier quietly removed the painting from the wall, carried it to a staircase, took off the frame, slipped the priceless artwork under his shirt, and left the museum.

"He hid the *Mona Lisa* in his Paris apartment for two years, but like most art thieves, Peruggia became frustrated when he couldn't sell it. In 1913, he smuggled the painting to Italy and offered it to a dealer with close ties to the Uffizi Gallery. The dealer contacted the museum director, and they tipped off the police. Peruggia was arrested when he arrived with the painting."

Fernandez was growing impatient. He wasn't concerned about the *Mona Lisa* heist. He needed Langstaff to focus on his immediate problem.

"Quint," he said. "How would you proceed with our missing Picasso problem?"

"Ah, Picasso." He grinned. "I heard about a guy at the Villages whose wife divorced him. He asked a friend to fix him up with a date. His friend obliged. The next day the guy called his friend and shouted, 'What kind of a guy do you think I am? That girl you fixed me up with was cross-eyed; her nose was long, thin and crooked; she had hair growing on her face; and she was flat chested.' His friend answered: 'Either you like Picasso, or you don't like Picasso.'"

Garcella Beauvoir exhaled loudly. She looked at her watch.

"Okay, let's get down to business," Langstaff said. "I did some checking last night. The original purchaser for Picasso's *Boy with a Pipe* was John Hay Whitney. He paid thirty thousand dollars in 1950. Whitney was the U.S. ambassador to the United Kingdom, publisher of the New York *Herald Tribune,* and president of the Museum of Modern Art; a man of unimpeachable character.

"The Picasso painting remained in Whitney's collection until it was sold. It was never loaned out except once, for a Picasso retrospective in 2002. In 2004 the painting was sold for one hundred four million dollars at a Sotheby's auction in New York. Sotheby's didn't name the buyer. My source said it was a Russian oligarch.

"Are you both still with me?"

Without waiting for a response, Langstaff continued. "The only window of opportunity for someone to swap the real Picasso with a forgery was when the painting was exhibited in Vero Beach—fifteen years ago."

"Where did you dig all this up?" Fernandez said.

"It took me twenty years—and fifteen minutes."

"Impressive," Garcella commented.

"As to your murdered guard," Langstaff asked Fernandez, "was he employed at the museum in 2002?"

"Yes."

"Security cameras?"

"Malfunctioning."

"Convenient."

"Have you looked into the guard's background?"

Fernandez shrugged. "Not yet."

"I would check out the victim's family and the entire museum staff. Run down every lead. You never know which one will pan out."

"If there *was* a switch in 2002," Fernandez said, "I can't believe Grace Carlyle's husband would have been stupid enough to hang a multi-million-dollar painting on the wall in his den."

"Why not? People assume stolen art has to be hidden away in some Swiss bank vault or a greedy collector's attic. What better place than displaying it in open sight?"

"If the art was worth millions," Garcella asked, "why wait fifteen years to go after it?"

"Good question." Langstaff handed her a piece of paper with a phone number. "Call this guy. Use my name. Ask for a background check on the deceased Mr. Carlyle and also on the museum's staff."

He checked his watch. "If we're going to grab lunch, Frank, we need to get moving. I want to be back at the Villages tonight."

The former head of the FBI's Rapid Deployment Crime Team turned to Garcella. "Nice meeting you, Captain. Be sure to keep a tight lid on this investigation. Secure your notes, and avoid the media. A powerful Russian oligarch was swindled out of a hundred and four million dollars. He won't be happy to learn about it. A word to the wise: don't tickle the nose of a sleeping bear. Those guys can play rough ... real rough."

...14

"STEER ME toward a cold Guinness and a handful of peanuts," Langstaff said. The two former FBI agents took seats by the rail at the Harbor Cove Restaurant and ordered beer. On the water's edge stood a cluster of palm trees, their fronds ruffling in the light breeze drifting off the Indian River.

A waitress took their food orders. Langstaff started with raw oysters, Fernandez with a shrimp cocktail. Both men requested the special of the day, grilled grouper in a basil-lime sauce.

"I remember hearing you took two slugs in the chest in a drug raid," Langstaff said. "I didn't mention it in front of the constabulary lady. How are you doing?"

"A couple of particles still stirring around. Doctor says to avoid physical exertion."

"Then why are you working—is it money?"

"I owed a favor to the former police chief."

Langstaff speared an oyster into his mouth. "Do you have a family here?"

"My wife and ... son live in St. Petersburg. We separated for a spell, but we're working it out."

"Why did you hesitate mentioning your son?"

"Long story." Fernandez dipped a piece of shrimp into the spicy sauce. "How about you? How did your family manage your traveling around the world tracking down art thieves and black-marketers?"

Langstaff ran his hands over his face as if to wipe the tiredness away. "Jeannie slipped into somebody else's bed—and never got out. She divorced me. As I told you on the phone, I have a live-in girlfriend. My two boys are married and have their own families. I see my grandchildren once every couple of years—if I'm lucky." He changed the subject. "Fill me in on your case."

"Three suspects with motive, means and opportunity."

"The unholy trinity."

Fernandez stopped and waited while the waitress put down their grouper platters.

"The robbery victim's son-in-law is a guy named Brad McCuskey, a former Navy SEAL. People imply McCuskey married the old lady's daughter for money. The guy has no regular job, owns a boat, and has no alibi for his whereabouts during the storm.

"The building maintenance man, Wilson, is also a person of interest. He has a sick wife and a daughter on drugs. Wilson was the last to leave the building before the hurricane. Like McCuskey, he had the access code for the Carlyles' unit. Also, Wilson lives on Hutchinson Island, so his movements weren't restricted by the bridge closings.

"Another suspect is Mrs. Carlyle's neighbor. His name is DeCicco. The neighbor and his wife left the building late, and he has reported Mafia connections."

"Have you interviewed him yet?"

"No. DeCicco's due back this week."

"In my experience, most art that gets stolen ends up in the hands of organized criminals. I told you and the chief about the Gardner Museum heist: a Vermeer, a couple of Rembrandts, five sketches by Degas, and more. I was convinced Italian-American gangsters in New England were behind the Boston robbery. In the world of organized crime, stolen art is frequently collateral for loans or currency in drug deals."

"I feel like I'm navigating through a fog," Fernandez said.

"If there *was* a swap and the Picasso original was replaced with a forgery, it raises two questions. Who had the means to cash out a hundred-million-dollar painting? Stealing is one thing, but trying to unload stolen artwork is another matter. I would look for someone with resources to unload the painting."

"You said it raised two questions."

"Since the switch involved a forgery, find the link—the forger. Unlike art thieves, forgers are driven by different motives. In addition to money, they're looking for fame, revenge on the establishment, or expression of their genius. Prison sentences tend to be light, and if forgers get enough publicity, it's worth a year or two in a minimum-security prison to then emerge as a kind of folk hero with a rewarding career."

"Going to prison doesn't sound like a career move," Fernandez said. He signaled the waitress for two more beers.

"I'll give you a good example: Heinze Meegeren. Meegeren tricked the art world into buying paintings in the style of Max Ernst, George Braque and Fernand Leger. One of his forgeries was accepted as an original and displayed at the Metropolitan Museum of Art in New York."

"Was he caught?"

"If you call it *caught*. I arrested Heinze Meegeren, and he served a short jail time. The truth is, I admired the guy's talent, and I even purchased a few of his paintings. After Heinze was paroled, I helped him get started in a legit business selling his art. Now he has a gallery in Delray Beach called Original Forgeries."

Fernandez narrowed his eyes. "No shit?"

"Meegeren knows what's going down in the underground art circles. Thanks to one of his tips, I recovered Matisse's *Odalisque in Red Trousers* for the Caracas Museum of Contemporary Art. The real Matisse had been swapped with a forgery years earlier, yet the museum's staff and curators, plus thousands of visitors, were unaware of the theft."

Langstaff flashed through his iPhone. "Heinze Meegeren is an invaluable source of 'off-the-reservation' information. If you're searching for the Picasso forger, he's your go-to guy. I'll alert Heinze to expect a call from you." He got to his feet. "But first I have to piss."

Somewhere to the south, a foghorn sounded two long notes.

* * *

WHEN LANGSTAFF RETURNED, Fernandez asked, "How do you tell if a painting's a forgery?"

"The quick answer is that good art is like porn; you know it when you see it."

"I think I can remember that."

"The more accepted approach," Langstaff said, "is utilizing a combination of provenance and scientific analysis. In its simplest terms, provenance is the historical record to authenticate a genuine work of art.

"For scientific analysis, they have scanners, color imaging equipment, digital X-rays, laser spectroscopy, and infrared reflectograms to look beneath the surface of the paint and see if there's an underdrawing. Forgers ordinarily don't use underdrawings. They tend to copy Dali, Chagall and

Picasso more often than Reubens, DaVinci or Velazquez, for practical reasons: it's easier to dab colors of paint on a canvas than to apply it with a smooth, seamless technique."

Fernandez remembered the painting on Avram Markus's wall. "You mention Chagall."

"I handled two Marc Chagall-related thefts. We nailed one of them. Actually, it fell in our laps. During a cocktail party at the Jewish Museum in New York in 2001, a one-million-dollar Chagall painting was plucked off the wall and smuggled out. The painting *Study for Over Vitebsk* depicted a man with a walking stick and a beggar's sack floating over Chagall's hometown of Vitebsk, Russia. We had no leads—*nada*.

"A year later the painting showed up in a post office in Topeka, Kansas. A postal employee opened the package because it was marked undeliverable. He saw museum stickers on the back of a painting. He went online and logged on to our FBI website for stolen art, saw the listing photograph, and contacted our FBI bureau in Kansas City. The painting is now back home in St. Petersburg, on display in the Russian Museum."

Fernandez smiled. "They should all be that simple."

"I struck out on the other Chagall case. The Bureau shut down my investigation."

"Why?"

He took a long pull on his beer. "As you know, Washington's a sieve. Word leaked that FBI Director Schreck and Vice President Landry hatched a plot in conjunction with Saudi Arabia, and without the President's knowledge, to force Israel to do our dirty work and marginalize Iran."

"What happened?"

"Schreck's body was found with two bursts in her chest and one in the brain. FBI agents questioned neighbors. No one heard or saw anything. It was not a random robbery gone wrong. Nothing was reported missing.

"A week later, Schreck's cleaning lady contacted our bureau to report that she'd noticed one piece of artwork had gone missing, a Marc Chagall oil painting. That's how I got dragged in. The odd thing was, the Chagall was Schreck's *only* uninsured artwork. It was unrelated to the murder, but a curious incident.

"At about the same time, Vice President Landry died of what was *reported* to be a heart attack."

"I remember." Fernandez nodded.

"Heart attack, my ass. Landry was visiting a homeless shelter on 16th Street in D.C. The V.P. was handing out gifts at a Christmas party when he collapsed. They rushed him to George Washington University Hospital, where Landry was pronounced dead on arrival."

"Why the cynicism?"

"When I interviewed the homeless shelter staff, I learned the last gift recipient greeted by Landry before his collapse was a disheveled-looking man with a cane."

"So?"

"The FBI forensic people got a look at Landry's body at the hospital before his last official act of lying in state at the Capitol Rotunda. Landry did die of a heart attack, but he had been injected with a deadly poison. The White House wanted to avoid a public panic: FBI Director executed, Vice President assassinated. My case was shut down. Justice sacrificed for the sake of expediency."

"Do you think the deaths were connected?"

"Payback for their meddling in the Middle East."

Fernandez remained sitting for a while after Langstaff left, staring into the distance. Something niggled at his memory, but he couldn't retrieve it.

The foghorn sounded again … like a dirge.

PART IV

THE FORGER

Mundus vuit decipi, ergo decipiatur.

The world wishes to be deceived, so let it be deceived.

...15

THE CELEBRITY FORGER cut a striking figure. Heinze Meegeren was a large, broad-shouldered man with a puffy red face, a halo of frizzy hair, and a Van Dyke beard. The artist wiped his hands on his smock and offered a brief handshake. He motioned Fernandez toward his workshop in the back of the gallery. His workroom reeked of turpentine, oil paint and varnish.

"Quint asked me to talk to you about a forged Picasso painting, *Boy with a Pipe*. I owe the man, so let's get this over with." The forger glanced at his watch. "The art establishment laments our so-called misdeeds, while at the same time they marvel at our skills. Forgery may be an economic crime, for which I have paid my dues, but it is not an artistic or aesthetic one. If a fake is good enough to fool experts, then it's good enough to give the public pleasure."

"No wonder your art gallery is doing well. You're a smooth hustler."

Meegeren said, "*Mundus vult decipi, ergo decipiator*."

"Meaning?"

"The world wishes to be deceived, so let it be deceived. Forgery isn't anything new," Meegeren explained. "Michelangelo created a sleeping Cupid figure, treated it with acidic earth to make it appear ancient, and then sold it to Cardinal Riario of San Giorgio. Many works by Titian, Rembrandt and Rubens were executed partly or mostly by their apprentices."

"That was a long time ago," Fernandez commented.

"I trust you're familiar with Andy Warhol? He freewheeled when it came to authenticity. You could never tell how much of a Warhol painting had actually been made by him versus some acolyte in his art factory."

"You guys are misunderstood, talented geniuses. Right?"

"Compared with greedy bankers, forgers never swindled people out of their homes and savings."

Fernandez stayed silent.

"Please don't misunderstand me. I love art, but this business of 'art for art's sake' is twaddle. It's a commodity, like gold or oil or pork bellies."

Meegeren picked up a three-by-four-foot oil painting. "*Whistler's Mother with Dog,* my top-selling creation.

"Thanks to Quint Langstaff, I got a second chance, and nothing illegal this time around. My paintings are clearly marked as fakes. It gives people a chance to avoid all the art-critic bullshit. I mean, one hundred million dollars for a Picasso painting of a kid with a pipe in his hand—that's absurd. Why don't these people give the money to fight global warming or build a new wing on the local hospital?"

"I agree," Fernandez said. "I'm investigating a robbery and a murder in Fort Pierce. A reproduction of Picasso's *Boy with a Pipe* was stolen during Hurricane Irma. A guard at the Riverside Art Museum in Vero Beach was a suspect in the heist—he was found murdered. Evidence points to the missing painting being an original Picasso that was swapped for a forgery in 2002 during a retrospective in Vero Beach."

"Anything is possible."

"Any ideas?"

A bell sounded in the gallery. Meegeren excused himself. "There's a coffee maker in the corner. Help yourself."

Fernandez checked his emails. Garcella Beauvoir had forwarded copies of PDF files of each of the museum's employees. He put off reading them.

Meegeren returned with a wolf grin, waving a check. "Van Gogh, Rembrandt, Gauguin and Modigliani all died in poverty. They should have taken up forgery."

The artist poured himself coffee and added a shot of bourbon. "Want some?"

"No thanks. How did you get started in—?"

"Started in forging paintings?" Meegeren finished the sentence. "In my early years I painted high quality art for galleries and then sat with my thumbs up my ass waiting for people to buy them. And then the gallery owners sold them and left me scraps. That's bullshit. I don't know about you, but when I get fucked, I want to enjoy it."

Fernandez smiled for the first time.

"I started combing flea markets and antique shops searching for old paintings of minor value. People were happy to unload crap lying around in attics or storerooms. The important thing was to locate paintings from the same period that I wanted to copy.

"I never made a direct copy of any artist. I borrowed elements and produced paintings that resembled their distinctive styles. That's why I never felt guilty duping gallery owners and art dealers. Some of them suspected something was up, but they made good bucks, and that was all that mattered to them."

"Weren't art dealers taking risks with you if they suspected the art was fake?"

Meegeren flashed a mischievous smile. "I had human nature on my side—greed. Collectors, museums and dealers don't advertise their gullibility."

"Did you copy Picasso's style?"

"I was more interested in Braque, Leger and Max Ernst. Picasso would have been easier to replicate. It just wasn't my thing."

"Whose thing was it?"

Meegeren looked closely at Fernandez. Then he laughed.

"Good segue, my friend. No. I don't know who produced the missing artwork you were asking about."

"I thought you were a friend of Quint Langstaff."

"I have a lot of friends." Meegeren chuckled. "Would you like a special price on a *Whistler's Mother with Dog*?"

"What I would like is to know who forged the *Boy with a Pipe*."

"Sorry. I cannot be of assistance."

"I don't have a lot of time," Fernandez pressed. "I'll ask you again, politely, and if that doesn't work, this will get unpleasant for you in a hurry."

Meegeren flinched and stared at his hands. "As unlikely as it sounds, there is yet honor among thieves."

"Consider your options. According to Quint, you have a popular TV show, standing room only for your Miami event, and a wealthy Delray clientele for original forgeries, correct?"

The artist blinked and nodded.

"As far as the Fort Pierce Police are concerned, you are withholding valuable evidence in a murder investigation. That makes you an accessory. I am prepared to leak this information to the media. How will your TV sponsors react? How will your fancy Delray patrons react?"

"That's bullshit. Nobody will believe it."

"Remember your Latin: *Mundus vult decipi, ergo decipiator*. If your TV sponsors and rich customers are deceived—so let them be deceived."

The color drained from his face. "You're a son of a bitch."

"And you're a scam artist. Now tell me who forged the Picasso, or get ready to shutter your gallery of fakes."

Meegeren coughed and cleared his throat. "Marie-Paul. Marie-Paul Lapére."

Fernandez waited for him to continue.

"Fifteen years ago, I was serving my sentence in 'Club Fed.' I heard through the grapevine Marie-Paul was strapped for cash. Her specialty was Picassos. She was the best. Some rich dude gave her a commission. Marie-Paul was paid to reproduce two copies of *Boy with a Pipe*. She delivered the forgeries and returned home to Bruges."

"*Two* Picassos?" Fernandez silently mouthed the word *Shit*.

"We're very different," Meegeren said. "You represent lawfulness. I have smaller aims, like making money and giving people aesthetic pleasure. Which of us helps other people more?"

Fernandez knit his brow and sighed. "How much for your *Whistler's Mother* knockoff—the one with the mutt?"

PART V

THE CON ARTIST

Caveat emptor.

Let the buyer beware.

...16

THE MAIN STREET OF DELRAY BEACH, Atlantic Avenue, was an eclectic mix of antique shops, clothing stores, gift stores and restaurants. Fernandez sat in Starbucks, drinking coffee. *Whistler's Mother with Dog* had been carefully wrapped and was propped up against his chair.

Fernandez reviewed the background information supplied by Quint Langstaff's contact. He started with Grace's husband.

Anthony Carlyle: Born 03-06-38, Baltimore, Md.
1974, Carlyle formed cosmetic company marketing hairdressing product to prevent baldness.
1977, Carlyle sued for false advertising. Court records reveal pomade consisted of animal fat: lard.
1982, Carlyle formed company to sell undeveloped land in Florida Everglades. Investors unable to inhabit marshy property. Building lots remain empty.
1995, Carlyle pleaded guilty to deceptive selling practices. He went bankrupt. Rumors circulated that Mafia money used in financing the land scam.
1999, Carlyle married wealthy widow, Grace Cushing. Carlyle became patron of art in Vero Beach. Wife was major donor to local museum, thereby assuring his selection as a board member in 2000.
2008, Carlyle heavily invested in stocks when market fell. Sought funding to recoup losses from unknown sources.
2012, Anthony Carlyle died in mysterious boat explosion off Vero Beach, Florida.

* * *

FERNANDEZ ordered another coffee and made a checklist of things to do. He knew that cases go cold quickly if momentum is lost. He had an uncomfortable feeling the hourglass was running out.

Carlyle's background check indicated Mafia involvement. He needed to connect with Mrs. Carlyle's neighbor, Vinnie DeCicco.

DeCicco picked up the phone after the first ring. "Yeah?"

"Mr. DeCicco, my name is Fernandez, I'm investigating the Carlyle break-in and the murder of—"

"Hold it, pal," DeCicco barked. "What's that got do with me?"

"Probably nothing, but I would like to meet with you and review—"

"Fuck off. I'm hanging up."

"I wouldn't advise you do that, DeCicco. We could conduct the interview at the police station instead."

"Don't threaten me. I grew up in New Jersey. My sister's married to a guy in the DeCavalcante family. You give me a hard time and your mother's going to start wondering why you stopped calling her."

"My mother died twenty years ago, wiseass. Listen up. I'll speak real slowly so you can understand me.

"We have new evidence," Fernandez lied, "about the mysterious death of Anthony Carlyle in 2012. The yacht explosion was an accident, right? Sure. Go tell your New Jersey relatives that if you don't cooperate in the Leroy Martin investigation, the Carlyle murder investigation will be front-page news. And there is no statute of limitation on murder. I'll be at your apartment at three o'clock. Be there. *Capisce?*"

Next, Fernandez scrolled Leroy Martin's sister's number and tapped the screen. The call went to her voice mail. He left a message.

Barbara McCuskey was third on his list. She picked up on the second ring.

"Good afternoon, Mrs. McCuskey. Frank Fernandez here. I'll be in your building this afternoon and would like to talk with your mother. Can you check and see if she has a few minutes for me?"

"Of course, Frank." Barbara McCuskey whispered in a sultry voice, "Why would I refuse you … anything?" She sounded like she had been drinking.

* * *

WAYNE GIBSON WAS ON DUTY at the Ocean Village gatehouse. The security guard motioned Fernandez to pull over.

"I remembered something about Leroy Martin; probably not important."

"You never know, Wayne. What do you have?"

"A few weeks back Leroy asked if I knew the name of a good jewelry store. I said if he was looking for a watch, there were great deals on the Internet. Leroy said it wasn't for him."

"Did you make a recommendation?"

"Kirk's Jewelers on Second Avenue."

"And did Martin take your advice?"

Wayne Gibson shrugged. "No idea."

Fernandez jotted down the information in his notebook.

* * *

VINNIE DECICCO WAS A SHORT, stocky man with a low belly, olive skin, dark eyes, and bushy black hair.

"I know how you guys work," he said. "You wearing a wire?"

Fernandez lifted his shirt and turned around.

"Satisfied?" he asked, as he depressed the "record" button on the iPhone in his pocket.

DeCicco grunted.

"Let me lay it out for you, Vinnie. I'm not interested in how Carlyle's boat blew up. The guy was a grifter. He owed the mob money and probably tried to palm off a forged Picasso painting as payment. Your people weren't stupid. They had the painting checked by experts and pulled the plug on Carlyle. It was just payback, right?"

DeCicco scratched his head and lapsed into silence.

"Here's the deal, Vinnie. I don't care about Anthony Carlyle. That's not my job, but nailing Leroy Martin's killer is. Understand?"

"Don't hammer me, man. Roy was my friend."

"Friend?"

"Shit, yeah. We fished together with McCuskey. Roy and Brad were asshole buddies. They were SEALs."

As Fernandez stood to leave, DeCicco shoved a business card in his hand. "If you got anymore bullshit questions, contact my lawyer."

* * *

FERNANDEZ TOOK THE ELEVATOR to Grace Carlyle's penthouse apartment and rang the bell. Barbara McCuskey answered the door.

"Coffee or something stronger?" she asked.

"No thanks. I need to be clear-headed. There are some odd twists in your mother's robbery case."

Fernandez studied Barbara McCuskey's well-shaped rear and let his imagination run loose for a few seconds. Then he took a deep breath and refocused his thoughts.

"I regret to inform you, Mrs. Carlyle, that your husband, Anthony, was engaged in a criminal activity. He commissioned two forgeries from a gifted Belgium artist in 2002."

Grace Carlyle reined in her emotions; her cigarette-husky voice was chilly and bone-dry. "Do tell."

"Your husband tried to palm off one of the forgeries on the Mafia for debts accrued, and the other fake he used to replace Jock Whitney's original Picasso on loan to the Riverside Museum. The original he hung in his den."

"Oh my God," Barbara McCuskey exclaimed.

"Mrs. Carlyle, the Picasso artwork was not taken from your apartment by mistake. And the jewelry heist was just a ruse to throw off suspicion. I believe the murdered security guard, Leroy Martin, was involved in a scheme to steal *Boy with a Pipe*."

Fernandez noticed a tremor in her hands. He continued, "Your husband's boat explosion was no accident. I must impress upon both of you not to discuss what I've told you with anyone. In addition to the Mafia connection, a Russian oligarch paid over a million dollars for the forgery. If news gets out prematurely, we could have a raft of problems we don't need."

"Why now?" Barbara McCuskey asked. "If the painting disappeared sixteen years ago, what triggered the break-in?"

"Good question. Someone learned the original was in your unit, or saw it there."

"Not likely," Mrs. Carlyle said. "I never entertain."

Barbara said, "The last time people were here in the apartment was Anthony's memorial service."

"Did you have a guest book for the service?"

"Yes, we did."

"May I borrow it?"

"Of course. I'll get it."

Fernandez said, "Mrs. Carlyle, I studied your husband's background. His hair cream was a scam using lard, and he bilked people in a Florida land scam. How could you not know your husband was a crook?"

Mrs. Carlyle looked for a moment as if she were about to burst into tears, but she took a deep breath and blew her nose instead. "Am I going to jail?"

Despite himself, Fernandez laughed. "As far as I know, you had no prior knowledge that your deceased husband was in possession of stolen merchandise; and if by chance you did know—*please* don't tell me."

"Anthony was no angel," Grace said, "but he was good to me. I'm not one of those women who think a man is the answer to everything. After my first husband died, I was tired of being alone. Anthony made me feel special." She brushed off a tear. "Companionship is a consolation when you're lonely."

Barbara returned with the memorial service guest log. "That man didn't love you, Mother. He was only after your money."

"Oh, for God's sake," Grace snapped back, "you shouldn't be the one to talk."

Fernandez felt weary. It had been a long and tiring day. "Remember," he said to both women. "This discussion is not to be repeated." He wagged a finger at Mrs. Carlyle and winked. "I don't think you would look nice in an orange jumpsuit."

"Whatever does it mean?" Grace Carlyle asked her daughter.

"It means I need another fucking drink."

* * *

DRIVING OUT THE GUARD GATE, Fernandez waved at Wayne Gibson. He was reminded of Leroy Martin and the jewelry store on 2nd Avenue. He checked his watch: 4:45. If he was lucky, they might still be open.

A man was preparing to hang metal storm panels, and a "closed" sign was on the door. Fernandez saw someone moving behind the counter. He tapped on the glass door. An elderly lady with large round glasses gave him a careful look before buzzing him in.

"I was closing up, but business is slow. I'm the owner, Clara Kirk."

Fernandez showed identification. "The Fort Pierce police are conducting a murder investigation, ma'am. The victim may have been a customer of yours."

"My gracious."

"Did a Leroy Martin make a purchase recently?"

Mrs. Kirk shrugged, tapped her head and chuckled, "As you get older, three things happen. The first is your memory goes, and I can't remember the other two. Please see that the door is locked. I'll check and be right back."

Fernandez looked over the display cases of assorted watches, rings and necklaces. He felt guilty. *When was the last time I bought Maris something nice*?

"I have it," Clara Kirk said, holding up a small metal-clasped envelope. "Mr. Martin placed his order on Friday morning, before the storm. I remember, because my husband was hanging plywood storm panels, and it was dark and hard to see.

"I was listening to the radio to learn if we would have to evacuate and try and find a motel somewhere inland. This man came in. He had nasty white scars on his face, but I've been in this business twenty-five years, and he didn't look threatening. Besides, my husband Jerry was right outside.

"Mr. Martin said he was a guard at the museum in Vero Beach. He picked out a simple emerald-cut diamond engagement ring and left a fifty percent deposit."

"Engagement ring? Was the ring engraved?"

"Young people just don't do that anymore," she said, shaking her head.

Fernandez shrugged. "Yeah. Unmarked rings fetch a higher price from pawnbrokers and online diamond buyers after a divorce."

Clara Kirk glanced at Fernandez's wedding band. "Is yours engraved?"

"Of course," he lied, feeling his face grow warm.

"Good for *you*!" Mrs. Kirk said with a thin smile. "Do you know who I should remit the deposit to?"

"I'll contact his sister and let you know. When was Mr. Martin planning to pick up his order?"

"He said he would pick up the ring the following week. He was waiting for his museum pension check to arrive."

* * *

SITTING IN HIS CAR, Fernandez telephoned Justin Williams' assistant.

"Ms. Adkins. Frank Fernandez here. Was Leroy Martin due a pension check from the museum?"

He heard a quick intake of breath, then silence. He thought they had lost wireless connection.

"Ms. Adkins. Can you hear me?"

"Yes. Yes. Of course I hear you." She sounded upset. "Our museum has no pension program for employees."

And the line went dead.

Fernandez's phone buzzed. He thought it was Margaret Adkins calling back. It was Lou Brumberg.

"How's the case coming, Frank?"

"It's still an active investigation—"

"Don't feed me that *active investigation* bullshit. It means you got nothing. I'm disappointed in you, Frank. I really am."

Fernandez felt Brumberg's criticism was justified. If the past few days had given him any perspective, it was that his FBI skill sets were well past their sell-by date.

PART VI

THE SUSPECT

"A hundred suspicions don't make a proof."

— Fyodor Dostoyevsky, *Crime and Punishment*

...17

IT WAS DARK WHEN FERNANDEZ arrived home. He fell into his battered leather chair and soaked in the gloominess of his mood. The number one suspect for Leroy Martin's murder was Brad McCuskey. Fernandez wanted to interrogate McCuskey, but he hesitated, having jumped the gun before and been proven wrong.

The call from Lou Brumberg made him feel guilty for procrastinating. He telephoned Garcella Beauvoir.

"Am I calling too late?"

"Yes," she grumbled. "Go ahead anyway."

"I think I know who killed Leroy Martin."

"I'm l-listening."

"It's all connected to the Carlyle break-in. Leroy Martin was a Riverside Museum guard. The way I see it, Anthony Carlyle involved Martin in a swap of the Picasso painting with a forgery in 2002. The motive was money.

"Martin needed to pay for his daughter's rehab in California. He told his sister he had pension money coming—not true. Martin recently ordered an engagement ring. He said he was *expecting* money in the near future to pay the balance of the deposit."

"Who was the woman Martin was buying the ring for?"

"No idea. Martin's trailer was an ash heap—no letters, fingerprints, nothing."

"Keep going."

"A guy named Brad McCuskey married Grace Carlyle's daughter for her money—"

Beauvoir cut in. "That's not a crime."

"McCuskey and Martin were Navy SEALs and fishing buddies. Martin had financial worries and a drinking habit. He probably shared his concerns with McCuskey and told him about Carlyle and the Picasso painting switch."

He heard an intake of breath. "*Probably* is not evidence."

"Bear with me, please. When I interviewed McCuskey, the guy was not too intimate with the truth. He wouldn't tell me where he was during the storm. He had a defensive, aggressive attitude and parried my questions in a way that suggested he knew the interview technique.

"As a SEAL, McCuskey was a trained killer. I think he masterminded the robbery, promised Martin money, killed him somewhere and dumped the body on Pepper Beach, assuming the storm would eliminate any traces.

"Then McCuskey tossed the jewelry into the river. He's a gold salvager. The stash would be safely hidden until he was ready to retrieve it, and gold never tarnishes in water. He didn't anticipate hurricane wave action would cause a shift in the sand toward Fisherman's Wharf. With Martin dead, there were no loose ends, and no one to share the proceeds of a sale of the original Picasso. I would like you to authorize bringing McCuskey in for questioning."

Garcella Beauvoir had a disapproving sound in her voice. "I've heard a lot of 'I thinks, ifs, and maybes.' You got a lot of probable and not much cause."

He remained quiet, waiting for her decision.

"Our investigation is looking a bit bleak," she admitted. "I don't see a down side, but no handcuffs—just talk. I'll have McCuskey brought in. Tomorrow, eight thirty. And don't be l-late, because I'm b-bumping a city councilman to get you in."

...18

THE MORNING SKY had a hazy quality. The weather was unseasonably warm for September. Garcella Beauvoir greeted Fernandez with a morose nod.

"McCuskey is in the interrogation room. I'll be listening on the intercom."

The tall, powerfully built man rocked back and forth in his chair, arms folded casually across his chest. He gave Fernandez a cocky smile.

One of Fernandez's FBI tradecraft instructors had told him that behavior always leaked. "There are clues," he had said. "Eyes blinking, the extra words wrapped around a simple yes or no answer, the cough, the meaningful pause. Behavior always leaks."

A table and two chairs took up most of the room. On the table was a time-coded recorder. Fernandez pushed the start button.

"Mr. McCuskey," Fernandez began. "You have the right to be represented by an attorney, but you have refused. Is that correct?"

McCuskey nodded.

"Please speak up."

McCuskey narrowed his eyes for a moment. "Yeah, no lawyer."

"My name is Frank Fernandez. The time is nine a.m. Wednesday, September 18th." He turned to McCuskey. "Please state your name, sir."

"Bradford McCuskey."

"What is your date of birth?"

"July 18th."

"What year?"

McCuskey grinned. "Every year."

There was an air of smugness in the way McCuskey answered. It gave Fernandez the urge to backhand the man across the mouth. As an experienced interviewer, he never showed irritation during an interrogation. McCuskey's attitude was testing his limit.

"You served in the Navy SEALs?" Fernandez asked.

"Correct."

"When?"

"'83 to '85."

"Where?"

"That's classified information."

"Do you have experience as a salvager working with Crown Jewels LLC, the company that owns the rights to dive on the wreckage sites off Fort Pierce?"

McCuskey's tone was icy. "In July and August I putter around offshore."

"You were a friend of Leroy Martin's?"

"Roy and I were SEALs."

"You fished together in your boat?"

"Right."

"You drank on board?"

"No law against it, is there?"

"Did your drinking *buddy* mention that the painting hanging in your mother-in-law's den was a very valuable painting by Pablo Picasso?"

After a moment of stony silence, McCuskey laughed. "You have to be joking."

"Didn't Leroy share with you his need for money and, after a few too many beers, didn't he brag about swapping a painting at the museum?"

Without waiting for a reply, Fernandez continued, "You saw an opportunity to cash in big-time. You enticed Leroy Martin to steal the painting during the storm and told him where Grace Carlyle kept her jewelry."

McCuskey suppressed a yawn.

"Then Sunday night you met Leroy, took the painting and jewelry, killed him, dumped his body on Pepper Beach and the jewelry in the river. You noted the GPS and, as an experienced salvager, you were in no rush to go after it, because it was safely stored under water."

McCuskey gazed at Fernandez, never once blinking.

"You have no witnesses to your whereabouts during the storm. I want the truth. Where were you?"

"I'm not obliged to answer your questions. But I will." He paused and looked at the recorder. "Keep it running."

There was a *gotcha* smugness in the way he spoke. "During the hurricane, I was with the St. Lucie County Search and Rescue Squad. Our team deployed Saturday night after Irma's winds lessened to tropical-storm-force gusts. We worked all night combing the Fort Pierce region for people in need. Sunday morning, we were transferred to help out in Okeechobee—all day. You want names of my rescue squad team?"

Fernandez flipped off the recorder. "I'll be right back."

As he entered the chief's office, Garcella gave him a tired smile. She had listened on the intercom.

"I fucked up."

"That you did. That you did. I'll come along while you try and make nice—and not get us sued."

They both entered the interrogation room.

"You're free to go," Garcella said. "Sorry for the inconvenience."

Brad McCuskey rose to leave. He glared at Fernandez. "You clueless bastard. How the fuck could you think I would kill a fellow SEAL?"

He stormed out, brushing Fernandez roughly aside with a sharp elbow to the chest. A painful twinge gripped him, like an iron claw squeezing his chest. He felt wobbly, the ceiling flashing before his eyes and spinning. Then his legs buckled and the alien darkness moved in.

...19

"ARE YOU AWAKE?" the man in the white coat asked. "My name is Dr. Chalasani. I'm a cardiologist. You suffered a mini-stroke, what we call a TIA, or transient ischemic attack. You were awake in the ambulance and provided telephone contacts for your wife and brother. We couldn't reach Mrs. Fernandez. Your brother agreed to get in touch with her and explain your condition."

"Which is?"

"As I am certain you're aware, Mr. Fernandez, you have lead fragments lodged near your heart. The recent trauma to your chest compressed those fragments against your heart muscle, causing a temporary blockage of blood flow to the brain. A TIA doesn't cause permanent damage, but ignoring it would be a big mistake."

"Why?"

"Two reasons. A TIA episode is a signal that a full-blown stroke may be ahead if your lifestyle doesn't change. Your brother informed me you underwent chelaton therapy to reduce the lead levels. Good.

"Nonetheless, you must avoid strenuous activities. No twisting, lifting or sudden moves. Those fragments are only five centimeters, or one and one-half inches, from your heart. A man of your age should begin to think about altering his lifestyle. Another heavy blow to your chest may kill you."

"Any other good news?"

"Yes. If you feel up to it, you may leave the hospital. Captain Beauvoir assigned a police officer to drive you home. I suggest you rest a day or two. As a result of your fall, you have abrasions on your chest and a bruised rib.

The nurse has your clothing and valuables and a two-day supply of Tramadol for pain—if needed."

*   *   *

ARRIVING HOME, FERNANDEZ FELT the painkillers lift him up to a dull euphoria. His cell phone buzzed. Maris. He let it ring. He wasn't up to hearing what he knew she had to say to him.

The phone rang again. It was his brother Martin.

"How do you feel?"

"Achy. I wasn't ready when the guy shoved me. It knocked the wind out of me. I'm fine."

"You're the only brother I'm likely to have," Martin said, "so please listen to me, Frank. With those souvenirs in your chest, you can't be fighting with people. Dr. Chalasani recommended having a pacemaker implanted in your chest to manage irregular heartbeats or arrhythmias in the event of another chest trauma."

Fernandez heard a noise.

"Someone's at the door. Let me get back to you."

Avram Markus appeared at the door. "I saw a police car transporting you home. I was concerned."

"All's well, thank you, Avram." Fernandez felt a vein throbbing in his forehead. He didn't invite the old man in.

"Well, I won't disturb you. Call if you need me."

Maris phoned again. She sounded out of breath. "Martin called. He said you had a mini-stroke. I contacted Lou Brumberg, and he called the police station. You got into a fight—didn't you?"

"It wasn't exactly a fight. I was interviewing a suspect in the murder case … and he had an aggressive attitude."

"Listen to me, Frank. I'm serious. When I agreed to quit the Dali Museum and come back to Fort Pierce, you made me a promise: no more John Wayne shit. I will not be a grieving widow of a man who insists on teasing fate, understand? That's not fair to me or to Charlie."

She hung up before he could respond.

...20

IT WAS RAINING WHEN FERNANDEZ woke up. A persistent rain drummed against the windows. He stayed in bed for a while, listening to the sound of the gusting wind. He was aware he was alone in bed. Sometimes being alone filled him with the sweet sensation of freedom—at other times with gloom and melancholy.

Fernandez got up to shower. As he was toweling off, he heard the doorbell ring. His first thought was that it might be Avram Markus again.

The doorbell sounded a second time.

Wearing a bathrobe, Fernandez padded to the door and looked through the peephole. Police Chief Garcella Beauvoir was holding an umbrella in one hand and a two-cup coffee container in the other.

He pulled the bathrobe tighter around him and opened the door.

"You take h-half and half and one Sweet'N Low, as I remember?"

He nodded, puzzled.

"Am I interrupting?"

"Come in. Come in. Give me your umbrella."

Beauvoir looked around. "Nice digs. In case the p-press shows up, you better put some clothes on."

"The press?"

"Word of the Leroy Martin murder leaked out."

As Fernandez headed for his bedroom, he heard her remark, "Nice legs."

* * *

WHEN FERNANDEZ RETURNED, the police chief was studying the tropical royal poinciana tree painting he had purchased from Willie Youngblood.

"Eye-c-catching," she said. "A local artist?"

"Willie Youngblood. He's one of the Highwaymen."

"Sounds like a bandit gang."

"Hardly. They're self-taught African-American artists. Rather than pick oranges, they took up painting. When no galleries accepted their work, they sold their stuff along roadsides—out of the trunks of their cars."

"My apartment could use some brightening up."

"Willie sells his art at the Farmers' Market."

Fernandez sat facing the police chief at his kitchen table. "Mind if I ask you a personal question?" she said.

"Depends on how personal."

"Why did Langstaff call you a saint?"

Fernandez took a long pull on his cold coffee. "In the good-old-boy FBI network of Ivy League alumni, loyalty prevailed over truth."

Garcella raised her eyebrows.

"You may recall in 1993 the Bureau of Alcohol, Tobacco and Firearms bungled a raid on a religious group near Waco, Texas. The FBI got into the act, and together with the Army, they mounted a fifty-one-day siege. According to official FBI documents, David Koresh's people ignited a suicidal pyre in which seventy-four people died—including twelve children."

"Damn," Garcella mumbled.

"A few years later, I was on assignment at Quantico and spotted cartons stored in a warehouse with no markings. As you know, I'm nosy. I opened a couple of boxes and found tapes and documents relating to Waco. I was surprised, because FBI officials had sworn in court that no such evidence existed."

"What did they say?"

"The first document I read reported that on April 19th, Army tanks rammed holes in the main Branch Davidian compound and pumped CS gas into the building."

"CS gas is a riot control agent," Garcella said.

"Right. At noon that day, two military pyrotechnic devices were fired into the structure. Those flash-producing projectiles sparked the fire that engulfed the compound in flames."

He paused. "It's hard to fathom, but Waco fire department trucks were prevented by the FBI from approaching the inferno. Then the burned-out ruin was razed in an attempt to remove evidence."

"What did you do?"

"I reported what I had found to my superiors. Word got to Attorney General Reno, who went public with the information. The exposure caused embarrassment and ruffled feathers throughout the bureau. I was singled out as the whistle blower, the virtuous but disloyal team player, ergo: Saint Fernandez."

"Since you are so public spirited," Garcella said, "m-maybe you can help me. I've scheduled a news conference today at noon at police headquarters." She exhaled. "Did you ever see the film *The King's Speech*?"

"The King of England had a speech impediment."

"As you may have noticed, I also h-have a problem."

Fernandez sipped his cold coffee. He offered her a careful smile.

"I was a street cop in Boston," Garcella said. "Then I earned a criminal justice degree at Bridgewater State University and ended up as police chief in Portland, Maine. Baltimore and Atlanta tried to r-recruit me. I turned them down. It's embarrassing to speak in public."

Fernandez intuited what was coming.

"Bottom line, I need your help. Please handle the press conference."

He took another swallow of coffee. "I'm in."

"Th-thanks. I'll have talking points typed up, in case you need them."

Quint Langstaff's warning flashed through his mind: "Don't tickle the nose of a sleeping bear."

Fernandez unwisely brushed it aside.

* * *

AT NOON, FERNANDEZ LOOKED OUT over the heads of journalists and the TV cameras gathered on the first-floor reception room of the police department. He noticed Lou Brumberg standing in the back of the room.

Garcella Beauvoir gave him the nod to begin.

Fernandez rapped lightly on the microphone with his pen. "Good afternoon, everyone. My name is Frank Fernandez. I am a former FBI agent, now retired. I have been retained by a group of ex-Navy SEALs to assist the Fort Pierce Police Department in their current investigation into the death of Leroy Martin. Chief Beauvoir and I are working closely together on the case.

"As background information, on Monday, September 11th, the body of Mr. Martin was discovered on Pepper Beach, North Hutchinson Island. The medical examiner concluded Leroy Martin had been murdered. The time of death was established at approximately eight p.m. Sunday, when Hurricane Irma was striking at full force in the Fort Pierce area."

Fernandez heard a low cough. Ben Herman raised his hand. "Frank. Why did the police department wait over a week before releasing this information?"

Herman was taking no notes, just standing against the wall. Fernandez remembered Ben Herman had an exceptional memory for details, for however long it took him to go somewhere and write it down.

"Hang on a minute, Ben. I'll get to that. Naturally, next of kin was notified." Fernandez continued, "During the storm, a robbery occurred in Ocean Village on Hutchinson Island. The reported theft consisted of valuable jewelry and one piece of artwork. We have reason to believe the murder of Mr. Martin and the robbery were connected. Leroy Martin worked two jobs. His day job was as a security guard at the Riverside Art Museum in Vero Beach, and his night job was as a part of the Ocean Village security detail."

Fernandez could see the reporters were growing impatient.

"Before opening to your questions, I want to respond to Ben Herman's question. We did not want to release information to the press until we were in a position to positively connect the robbery to the murder."

He heard disgruntled sounds from the audience.

A woman reporter with a reedy voice called out, "What was the painting?"

"I'm getting to that. Tuesday, September 16th, a fisherman on North Hutchinson reeled in a portion of the missing gold jewelry. Police divers have since recovered the balance of the items reported stolen. This led us to conclude that the missing painting, not the jewelry, was the primary objective of the robbery."

"Who killed Martin?" one reporter asked.

"We can't comment on that at this time."

"Why was the jewelry dumped in the river?"

"While the jewelry may not have been the principal motive, it is possible the thieves stashed the jewelry in the river for safekeeping until they were ready to retrieve it. Gold does not tarnish when exposed to water."

"What was the painting?" the woman with the reedy voice repeated.

Ben Herman spoke up. "My sources tell me it was Picasso's *Boy with a Pipe*. Is that correct?"

Fernandez nodded with a forced smile.

Herman continued. "*Boy with a Pipe* sold at auction at Sotheby's for over one hundred million dollars."

A quiet gasp spread through the room.

"We can't comment on that at this time," Fernandez said again, "but we have reason to believe a conspiracy took place years ago, resulting in the original Picasso painting being stolen from the Riverside Art Museum in Vero Beach — and replaced with a forgery."

The Channel Five TV reporter asked, "Have you recovered the original Picasso painting?"

"We're working on positive leads," Fernandez lied.

He caught a glimpse of irritation in Ben Herman's eyes. Herman had the journalistic instinct. He could sniff news and home in on it.

"Do you know who switched the paintings?" a voice called out.

"Yes. A man named Anthony Carlyle."

"Has Mr. Carlyle been apprehended?"

"Mr. Carlyle is deceased."

"Wasn't Carlyle killed in a boat explosion?" Ben Herman queried.

"I can't comment on that at this time."

Fernandez could feel his tiredness seeping through, once the adrenaline rush of being on television had faded.

Garcella Beauvoir rose and went to the microphone. She cleared her throat. "Th-thank you all for coming. We will r-remain in close touch with the media."

* * *

AFTER THE ROOM CLEARED, Garcella said, "Maybe you overdid the 'We can't comment at this time' variations, but the truth is we've got no suspects, no weapon and no evidence."

Fernandez's cell phone vibrated and chimed in his pocket. He had turned it off before the press conference. It was Brumberg.

"That press conference was one big yawn. Over a week and you've got nothing? On top of that, my people are pissed. You accused Brad McCuskey of murdering a brother SEAL."

Fernandez didn't know how to respond.

"Bottom line, Frank. The men want you to know that if you can't find Leroy's killer—ring the bell and quit. Sorry, pal. That's just how it is."

After he hung up, Fernandez looked at Garcella. "I've been put on a short leash. Brumberg's SEAL buddies expect results—not excuses. They want me to ring the bell and quit if I can't handle the job."

"Ring the bell?"

"SEALs go through a Hell Week of brutal tasks with little sleep. At headquarters they have a bell. If the misery gets to be too much, a trainee can opt out and ring the bell."

"Are you ringing the bell?"

"Not yet. I'm going to cast a wider net. I need to find the woman Martin was going to marry, talk to Martin's sister again, and review the background checks on the museum personnel."

Fernandez checked his watch: three p.m. He felt a slight discomfort under his right ribcage. His phone chimed again.

Ben Herman said, "I checked. The anonymous purchaser of *Boy with a Pipe* was Grisha Chuychenko, a hard-ass Russian oligarch with close ties to Putin."

"Thanks Ben. That's good to know."

"Maybe, maybe not. You took center stage when you announced publicly that *you* had positive leads on the missing Picasso painting. I'm advising you, as a friend, to be careful, Frank—very careful."

...21

LATER THAT EVENING Fernandez sat alone at his desk, eating a slice of cold pizza with one hand and scribbling a list for himself with the other. He began the process of reviewing Riverside Art Museum's personnel files. He began with Executive Director Justin Williams.

Born: June 13,1947, Boston, Mass.
1968-71: Undergraduate degree: Parsons School of Design, New York City
1972-74: Master of Fine Arts Degree (MFA), Parsons-New School.
1975: Crater/Fine Art Handler. U.S. Art Co., Randolph, Maine.
1976-78: Instructor-Rhode Island School of Design, Providence, RI.
1979-1983: Asst. Director-Joslyn Art Museum, Omaha, Nebraska.
1983-85: Asst. Director-Art Gallery of Victoria, British Columbia, Canada.
1986-94: Director-Winnipeg Art Gallery, Winnipeg, Manitoba.
1995-99: Executive Director, Arkansas Arts Center, Little Rock, Ark.
2000-2008: Self-employed-International Fine Art authenticator.
2009: Authored *The Fine Art of Provenance*
2010: Executive Director, Riverside Museum of Art, Vero Beach, FL.

Fernandez noted that Williams had moved around a lot professionally. Nothing else sparked his interest.

When his phone rang, it was Leroy Martin's sister returning his call. Becky Foster's voice sounded strained and distant. "Any news?"

"No. But I am still working the case full time."

"We buried Roy yesterday. It was a lovely ceremony. The pallbearers were SEALs from the Naval Amphibious Base in Virginia Beach. Roy was a recipient of the Silver Star in 'Nam, so the Navy permitted his burial at the Naval Academy Cemetery in Annapolis."

In an unsteady voice, Becky Foster continued. "They did the whole bit with the Academy honor guard firing the volleys and the sound of the bugler's taps echoing off the Severn River—"

He heard a sob and a sad sigh.

"I have good memories of Roy: his sense of humor, his kindness, his love of art. Gone. Just like that—gone. All I have to remember Roy are the few paintings he gave me—from Parsons."

"Parsons?"

"When he was nineteen, Roy was offered a scholarship to Parsons School of Design in New York City. After two years, he quit to become a Navy SEAL and was sent to Vietnam. My poor brother ended up an alcoholic with a frozen face seamed with scars, a post-traumatic stress disorder, and a sidelined career. What a waste."

"I'll do whatever I can, ma'am."

"Thank you, Mr. Fernandez. You sound like a decent man. As soon as I can, I'll write thank-you notes to the folks who sent flowers: the people from the SEAL Museum and Roy's lady friend."

"Lady friend?"

"Margaret."

After he disconnected, Fernandez thumbed through Margaret Adkins' personnel folder. It noted her husband Edgar had died of cancer five years earlier. Fernandez shook his head. He had missed it. He jotted a note to contact Margaret. Maybe she could shed some light on the investigation.

Fernandez had the feeling he was also overlooking something else. But he couldn't pin it down. He felt weary and needed to close his eyes for a few minutes. He had had enough for one day.

* * *

AT ONE A.M., Fernandez bolted upright.

"Parsons," he mumbled, flipping on the desk light, searching for Williams' file.

He exhaled loudly. "Damn, damn, damn. Was it a coincidence? Could Justin Williams and Leroy Martin have attended Parsons School of Design at the same time?"

He reread Williams' file: 1968-71: Undergraduate degree, Parsons School of Design. 1972-74: Master of Fine Arts Degree (MFA), Parsons-New School.

Fernandez mused aloud. "If Leroy Martin served in Vietnam in 1973, it's possible he attended Parsons two or three years earlier. That's *it*. That's fucking *it*. Williams and Martin were *connected*."

He threw a pod in the coffee maker. On a legal pad, he jotted questions that needed answering: Did Williams mastermind the Carlyle theft and murder Leroy Martin? Why was Leroy Martin involved—what motive? How did

Williams know the original Picasso *Boy with a Pipe* was in the Carlyle apartment? Where was the painting now? And how would Williams plan to dispose of it?

Fernandez drained his coffee, reflecting. Williams' personnel file indicated he had been an international fine arts authenticator. He probably had connections to sell the painting. Leroy Martin had a daughter in an expensive drug rehab and was planning on getting married. He needed money. And Leroy Martin had probably told his college friend Williams about swapping the original Picasso painting for a forgery.

He rifled through his desk until he found Anthony Carlyle's memorial log. As expected, Justin Williams had attended and had the opportunity to view the Picasso painting.

Fernandez couldn't afford another screwup like the McCuskey interview. Garcella had cautioned him, "*Probably* is not evidence." There were coincidences that connected Justin Williams to the crimes, but hard evidence was needed before he could confront the museum director.

Fernandez had never believed in coincidences—neither did he dismiss them.

PART VII

RETRIBUTION

"Vengeance and retribution
require a long time; it is the rule."

—Charles Dickens, *A Tale of Two Cities*

...22

IT WAS AFTER ELEVEN P.M. when Justin Williams heard the rap at his door. He cautiously peered through the peephole but couldn't see clearly. The front door light was malfunctioning—for some reason.

As Williams opened the door, he stared into the muzzle of a Beretta silencer.

Justin Williams barely heard the short pops of two 9 mm bullets—aimed directly at the center of his heart.

The museum director stumbled backwards, hands groping his ruined chest before his knees buckled and he crumpled dead to the floor.

...23

"ANOTHER CLEAR, SUNNY DAY on the Treasure Coast," the chirpy weather girl said. "Highs expected in the eighties, with a chance of rain in the afternoon."

As Fernandez stabbed at his plate of eggs, a more serious voice announced, "Late breaking news: murder in Vero Beach coming up next—stay tuned."

He turned up the volume.

WPTV-Channel Five's anchorman appeared on screen. "Local police are investigating the shooting death of Justin Williams, executive director of the Riverside Art Museum in Vero Beach. A home cleaning crew discovered Mr. Williams' body early this morning in his Fort Pierce residence. More after this brief commercial."

Fernandez exhaled sharply. He dug out Garcella's private number.

"Beauvoir," she answered.

"What the hell's going on?"

"Can't talk, I'm at the crime scene."

"Why wasn't I notified?"

"Emerson is handling the case."

"But Garcella, Williams' murder is connected to—"

She had hung up.

Fernandez was tempted to call her back and share the link between Williams and Martin. He hesitated, not wishing to be embarrassed again.

He decided to reread Justin Williams' background information. In 1975 Williams had worked for a company in Maine specializing in wood crating of fine artwork. Fernandez thought it possible Williams had crated, relabeled and stored *Boy with a Pipe* either in his home or in the temperature-controlled art museum.

When he telephoned the museum, a recorded message announced that the Riverside Museum of Art was closed due to the untimely death of the executive director. He booted up his computer and tapped in "Riverside Museum of Art."

> **VERO BEACH, FL**. Jan. 2010. Riverside Museum of Art Board of Trustees Chairperson Lesley Gilman announced the selection of Justin Williams as the museum's new Executive Director/CEO. Mr. Williams had formerly been chief curator at the Arkansas Art Center.

Fernandez found Lesley Gilman's number in the phone directory. He called her.

"Ms. Gilman, my name is Fernandez with the Fort Pierce police department. I'm working the murder case involving your deceased security guard … and the missing Picasso painting."

"Yes. Yes. Terrible. Our director has been murdered."

"Ma'am. We have reason to believe the missing painting was wrapped, mislabeled and possibly concealed in your museum. I need to make an inspection—"

"Impossible! I will not permit police tramping around our museum, especially on a day like this."

"I understand your concern. However, we're dealing with one or more murders and a missing multi-million-dollar painting. I could get a search warrant. How will that look in the newspapers: museum refusing to cooperate in major art theft and murder investigation?"

He heard a sharp intake of breath. "You are an unpleasant person, mister whatever your name is."

"Have a security guard meet me at the front entrance in one hour. My name is Fernandez."

* * *

"I'M THE GUY YOU'RE LOOKING FOR," the museum guard grunted. "Cliff Lewis." Lewis was in his sixties, squat and built like an aging ballplayer. His voice was deep, calm and measured. He took his cap off and ran a hand through his thinning gray hair.

"I'm working with the Fort Pierce Police Department," Fernandez said. "We have reason to suspect a missing Picasso painting may be stashed in the museum."

"Not much art stored here. No space."

Fernandez pressed, "Well, let's give a look. The painting is about 32 by 39 inches. If it's crated, the size would be about three by three and a half feet."

The two men completed a close inspection of storage areas and found nothing. "I need a quick look in Justin Williams' office," Fernandez said.

"I'm afraid I can't do that. Fort Pierce Police ordered the office sealed until they get here."

"Was it Detective Emerson who called?"

Lewis shrugged. "Didn't get his name."

"You were Leroy Martin's friend."

"That's true."

"I'm trying to find out who killed him."

"I know. I saw you on TV. You're ex-FBI, right?"

"What was your opinion of Justin Williams?"

"The guy was a self-righteous prick."

"Help me out, Cliff. Five minutes in and out."

"I'm due to retire. I don't need problems. Know what I'm sayin'?"

Fernandez handed the guard a fifty-dollar bill. "Go get coffee."

A hint of doubt darkened Lewis' face. "Five minutes —that's it."

Donning plastic gloves, Fernandez checked the computer on the console behind Justin Williams' desk. It was password protected.

Williams' desk was locked.

From his pocket Fernandez extracted a paper clip and knife. He used the screwdriver on his Swiss Army knife to put pressure on the top-drawer lock and then raked the pins with the paper clip to get the tumbler to turn. Once the desk drawer was open he fished around, found a small black address book, and slipped it into his pocket.

He had no idea why. Instinct.

...24

ON IMPULSE, FERNANDEZ TELEPHONED Garcella Beauvoir. His call went to her voice mail; the police chief was avoiding him. He called the station and requested Floyd Emerson's cell phone number.

When Emerson answered, he said. "Fernandez here. Quick question. Was Justin Williams' house thoroughly searched?"

"Yeah, why?"

"No hidden areas large enough to store a three-foot wooden crate?"

"You watch too much TV." Emerson disconnected.

Idly, he thumbed thru Justin Williams' black address book. Fernandez didn't know what he expected to find. No names looked familiar. Flipping through the book, one name attracted his attention: Lisa Rodriguez.

Fernandez pressed REDIAL. He called Emerson back.

"Jesus. What now?"

"Was the cleaning woman who found Williams' body named Rodriguez?"

"So?"

"Thanks, Floyd."

Don't dismiss coincidences, he mused. Lisa Rodriguez had provided a cleaning service for both Justin Williams and Grace Carlyle. She was in and out the Carlyle apartment. The value of the Picasso painting was now public knowledge. If Williams had hidden the painting in his home, Lisa's cleaning crew might have happened on it—and an opportunity presented itself.

He checked Williams' address book and tapped in Lisa's number.

"Rodriguez Cleaning Service."

"Lisa, this is Frank Fernandez. We met at Mrs. Carlyle's apartment."

"Did you want to schedule a cleaning?"

"Your crew discovered Williams' body, right?"

After a long pause, she said, "Yes, sir. It was terrible."

"Are you at home?" Fernandez asked.

"I was too upset to work today."

"I understand. You take it easy, Lisa. Bye."

* * *

LISA RODRIGUEZ'S HOME WAS A TIDY, one-story rancher painted dark gray with white trim along the gable roof. Yellow hibiscus lined the front of the house.

When Fernandez pressed the doorbell, he saw the dull flicker of television through the front window. After several minutes, the door was opened and the screen unlatched. A young girl looked out at him.

"I need to speak with Lisa."

She began to object. "My mother isn't—"

Fernandez flashed his investigator badge.

"It's okay, Debby. Let the man in."

After the TV was turned off, Lisa Rodriguez gave him a wan smile. "Hello, Mr. Fernandez. It's been a rough day, finding the man's body and all."

Fernandez decided to press the issue. "It's better if you talk to me, Lisa, and not the police. Where is it?"

She gaped at him. Her face flushed red. "What—?"

"You have family in Puerto Rico, right?"

"That's not a crime."

"How did they make out after the hurricanes?"

"No power. No food. No place to live," she said heatedly. "FEMA's telling CNN relief efforts are going well. That's bullshit. They're lying about the number of dead people. My family has yet to see a National Guard, FEMA, Red Cross or federal vehicle anywhere."

Fernandez nodded in silent agreement.

"If the government don't treat Puerto Ricans as citizens with equal rights, then we look after our own—any way we can."

"You can't look after your family from a jail cell." Fernandez touched her shoulder. "I can help, but you have to trust me."

Lisa shook her head. "No thanks."

"Did you think you could pawn a hundred-million-dollar painting?"

Lisa shrugged.

"The FBI will be crawling all over you and your family. And so will the U.S. Immigration and Customs Enforcement Agency."

At the mention of ICE, Lisa's face froze. Fernandez guessed some members of her cleaning crew were undocumented immigrants.

Lisa's head angled slightly as she considered her options. She took in a deep, shaky breath, let it out, and nodded. "Do I need a lawyer, Mr. Fernandez?"

He suppressed a smile. "Call me Frank. Nobody calls me Mr. Fernandez. I need you to answer my questions and follow my instructions."

She nodded.

"When your crew was cleaning Williams' home, you stumbled on the missing painting."

"Yes."

"Was it crated?"

"Bubble-wrapped."

"Let me have the painting. I'll tell the police you saw the artwork while cleaning Williams' home. You contacted me because I was the one who interviewed you about the Carlyle robbery. And then we all try as best we can to live happily ever after."

"Debby, get the ... package."

"*Gracias*," Fernandez said.

Lisa Rodriguez whispered, "Williams was creepy. When you clean a person's house, you get a feeling about the customer."

"Such as?"

"I didn't like the way he looked at my daughter."

* * *

THE BUBBLE-WRAPPED PAINTING was carefully enclosed in a blanket and secured in Fernandez's trunk. He tapped in Quint Langstaff's number. When the ex-FBI art investigator answered, Fernandez explained he had recovered Picasso's *Boy with a Pipe*.

Instead of offering a pat on the back, Langstaff sounded concerned. "Listen up, Frank. You're carting a hundred-million-dollar work of art. Return the painting to the museum ASAP. It's their responsibility to sort out legal ownership."

"The museum is closed due to the ... murder of their executive director—"

"Ah, shit. You didn't mention that tidbit. I suggest you head directly to the Fort Pierce police station. Don't stop to eat or piss. Have the Picasso painting photographed and locked in the police evidence room, get a damned receipt and be done with it."

"Aren't you being a little over-dramatic?"

"Don't be an asshole, Fernandez. While you were sharpening pencils in your fancy office in the Hoover Building, I was on the street, working undercover. And I survived by staying out of the limelight, and not having a bullseye painted on my back."

* * *

"PRESENTO. YOUR MISSING PICASSO," Fernandez said, hoisting the bubble-wrapped painting onto the police chief's desk.

Garcella seemed underwhelmed. "I'm busy, over-caffeinated, constipated, and weary from lack of sleep," she said. "You handle it."

"This Picasso is worth mega millions," Fernandez said. "Langstaff advised us to secure it under lock and key until it can be returned to the museum. I need you to witness my surrendering it. Please."

Fernandez lifted the package and carried it through the lobby into the evidence room. With scissors, he carefully removed the bubble wrapping and stood silently studying Picasso's *Boy with a Pipe*.

The face in the painting had an unblemished look, with a beautiful crown of roses positioned over the boy's head, contrasting with his dirty overalls. Fernandez was surprised at the effect the painting had on him—almost a physical impact.

He noticed Garcella staring at the painting with a troubled expression.

"You don't seem impressed."

"I'm not a Picasso fan."

"Isn't he the greatest artist of the 20th century?"

"He was a misogynist."

"I don't even know what *misogynist* means."

Garcella Beauvoir's face darkened. "It means the bastard mistreated women. He got away with it—like most powerful men—because he *could*. Picasso was a creator of art, but a destroyer of women. Of the most important women in his life, two killed themselves and two went mad. Another died within four years of their relationship. Do you want names and dates?"

Her words were as sharp as a slap in his face.

Fernandez fell silent, and the silence spun out. He felt his face turning red with embarrassment.

Garcella Beauvoir stormed out of the room.

* * *

LATER THAT EVENING, Fernandez sat in Archie's Seabreeze Restaurant, idly watching the wind rustling palm trees as the September sky darkened over the ocean. Bolts of lightning began to spark in the far distance. The rain would begin soon.

He signaled Janice for a beer and a hamburger. On the TV behind the bar, the Marlins were losing to Cincinnati. He wanted to finish eating and get home before the storm.

"Well, well," he heard Floyd Emerson say in a mocking tone. "The famous *Señor* Fernandez, publicity seeker and tracer of lost masterpieces."

A gloomy silence settled over the bar.

The whites around Emerson's eyes were marbled—he'd been drinking.

"Let it go, Floyd. This isn't the time or place."

"I hear McCuskey kicked your ass."

They held each other's cold stares for a long moment, neither man blinking. Finally Fernandez spoke.

"I'm sorry about your family problems, Emerson—"

"Fuck you, Fernandez," he said bitterly. "At least my wife's not putting out—"

The words were hardly out of Emerson's mouth when four rigid fingers jabbed into his solar plexus. He was taken by surprise, grunting in pain. Fernandez followed with a short straight fingertip just below the ear. Emerson's head jerked up and his mouth fell open. He crumpled onto the sandy floor.

Fernandez pushed his beer away, preparing to leave.

The lightning display faded into a steady rain.

Janice handed him his tab. "Don't miss our church service, Frank—tomorrow, nine a.m. Truly inspiring."

...25

FOR FERNANDEZ, SLEEP WAS long in coming that night. It was after midnight before he nodded off. He was wakened by insistent phone chimes. Fernandez ignored them, hoping to get a little more sleep, but the number continued to call back. The gray light of dawn had begun to creep in through the window. It was a few minutes past seven.

"A barroom brawl." Garcella Beauvoir's voice sounded strained to the point of near breathlessness. "Emerson's been suspended. He's off the force. And your presence is also no longer welcome."

All Fernandez could do was mumble his apology, but the line was dead.

He walked to the window. The sky was overcast. A thick cloud of fog had replaced last night's rain. Fernandez turned on the kitchen light to make coffee. When the phone rang again he hoped it was Garcella calling back, a little calmer.

The caller was Lesley Gilman, chairwoman of the board of the Riverside Art Museum. "Mr. Fernandez. I understand *our* Picasso has been recovered."

Before he could reply, Gilman continued in an officious voice. "I'm calling to arrange transfer of the painting to our museum location."

"Hold on a moment, lady. You need to call the Fort Pierce police. I'm out of the loop. Ask for Captain Beauvoir. The painting is in the station's evidence room."

Ms. Gilman conducted a muffled conversation with someone.

"Well, there *is* another matter. If the investigation drags on and on, our board feels it will place a worrisome cloud over the museum and our donors."

"Understandable."

"Our security guard, Mr. Lewis, advised the board that you had served with the FBI. And according to the media, you were the person responsible for locating the stolen Picasso."

"Yes, ma'am." Fernandez could tell Lesley Gilman teetered on the verge of an apology but decided not to bother. He knew what she wanted.

"The board authorized me to contact you to in regard to investigating Justin Williams' murder."

"I'm available."

"And what is the cost of your ... service?"

"One hundred dollars per hour, plus expenses."

"How soon can you start?"

"I already have."

Fernandez felt his adrenaline kick up a notch. He knew the murdered security guard, Leroy Martin, had been planning to marry Margaret Adkins. If Adkins had discovered that it was her boss, Justin Williams, who had killed Martin, she would have had a strong motive—revenge. In addition, Williams wouldn't have felt threatened if his assistant showed up at his door late at night.

Fernandez called. Margaret Adkins agreed to see him and provided the entrance gate code for the Atrium, a twelve-story oceanfront condominium complex.

Margaret Adkins opened the door. "I guess you're curious how a museum secretary can afford the Atrium."

"The thought crossed my mind."

"My late husband Karl did very well when he sold his clothing store chain. I love art and needed something to occupy my time and my mind. You know, an idle mind is the devil's workshop."

"So I've heard, Mrs. Adkins."

"Margaret."

"Okay. Margaret. Leroy Martin's sister said you attended the funeral in Annapolis."

"Yes. I had a fondness for Leroy."

"A fondness?" Fernandez raised an eyebrow. "Weren't you two planning on getting married?"

"Dear me. No." She laughed. "Leroy kept me company, if you know what I mean. We all have needs."

"Didn't he buy you an engagement ring?"

"Oh, the ring. I told Leroy to return it to the jeweler or to have it reset for his daughter. She lives out west."

"Margaret. The museum hired me to investigate the murder of your former boss. I'm a state-licensed private investigator. But I was in the FBI for twenty years. I need to ask you some questions."

"Please, go right ahead."

"Did Leroy Martin confide in you that he and Justin Williams conspired to remove the Picasso painting from Mrs. Anthony Carlyle's home?"

"Of course not, but I felt Justin wielded undue influence over Leroy."

"What was your opinion of Justin Williams?"

"I'd rather not say."

"I'm investigating his murder. It could be important."

"I won't speak ill of the dead."

Fernandez took out his notebook. "Do you mind telling me where you were Friday night?"

"Well, let me see. Leroy's funeral was Thursday afternoon. Other than his sister and the Navy people, no one else attended. From now on, the only person who will know Leroy's name is whoever mows the grass near his headstone."

Fernandez sensed she was avoiding his question.

"Friday night," Fernandez repeated. "You were telling me where you were Friday night."

"Yes. We left Annapolis Thursday afternoon—"

"We?"

"My daughter Sarah helped with the driving."

Fernandez did the math. He knew the driving distance from Washington to Vero Beach was 1000 miles, or about 16-18 hours' drive time. He estimated even if Margaret and her daughter had stayed at a motel on I-95, she could have easily made it back in time to avenge her friend's murder.

"I presume you stopped at a motel Thursday night."

"The Hampton Inn outside of Richmond."

"And you arrived back in Vero Beach before dark?"

Margaret gave him a troubled glance. "You think I left Leroy's funeral and high-tailed it home so I could kill my boss, Justin Williams?"

"It's my job to—"

"It's not your job to insult me. Friday night I stayed at my daughter Sarah's house in Jacksonville. You can interrogate my little granddaughters if you like. Give them lie-detector tests—they'll love it."

Her eyes were locked on Fernandez's. "I think you should go."

Fernandez tried to mumble an apology. "I admit I was wrong."

"Leave now," Margaret said, "or I'll call security."

He nodded his contrition and left.

From the apartment next door, a gray-haired woman briefly appeared and fish-eyed Fernandez. She raised her eyebrows and smirked. "You the new one?"

...26

THE FLAT, TONELESS MESSAGE on his answering machine reminded Fernandez of his appointment with Dr. Chalasani to schedule a pacemaker implant. He sat at his desk, looking at his father's photograph. It prompted him to call his brother.

"Dad's lost a lot of weight," Martin Fernandez said. "And he looks tired all the time, but the meds are keeping him calm. I don't know how much time—"

"I'm on a case, a murder case, Martin. Maybe I can get up there next week."

"Okay," his brother said, changing the subject. "How are *you* feeling?"

"I'll probably get the pacemaker put in."

"One night in the hospital and you're good to go."

"Say hi to Dad. I'll try my best to get there soon."

"Don't wait too long, Frank. He's headed into the fog —and soon."

Fernandez remembered the last visit to Baltimore after Luis had suffered his heart attack. That visit was the first time he had seen the man in years. Luis' white hair was thinning, and his frame looked fragile.

"How you doing, Pop?" Fernandez had asked.

"They got me walking around in this gown with my ass hanging out."

"You're a sly old fox. I'm staying in your apartment; last night I found a cigar box full of medals. I didn't know you were wounded and earned the Purple Heart. Why didn't you ever tell me?"

"I got the medals, but I also got the aches and pains and wintertime tingle from frostbite."

"Maybe when you get out of the hospital and finish physical therapy, you'll move to Florida? There's an apartment available in my building, and … I can keep an eye on you."

"Nice of you to ask, Frank," his father said. "I don't think so. My doctors are here at Hopkins."

"There are top-notch cardiologists in Fort Pierce."

"What does it cost to live down there? I don't want to outlive my money."

"Not to worry. Martin and I will handle the finances."

"I hate the fucking cold weather," Luis said. "It goes right through me. Reminds me of Chosin Reservoir."

Fernandez was silent.

"Martin's been a good son; he and his wife have me over every week. I don't want him to feel I don't appreciate it. And *his* kids are likely the only grandchildren I'll ever have."

He had ignored the barb and said, "Martin and his family can come and visit. Disney World and the Kennedy Space Center are only a few hours away. Martin loves fishing. Fort Pierce is big on fishing."

"Yeah, but what the hell would I do?"

"I live a block from the harbor. Every Saturday there's a farmers' market where you can get fresh produce and good Mexican food, and across the street from our condo is Veteran's Park, a nice place to sit and enjoy the warm weather."

"You sprung this on me kind of sudden. I need to think about it."

"You do that, Dad."

"Tell you the God's truth," Luis said. "Living alone sucks."

He could see his father was tiring. Fernandez remembered kissing the old man's forehead and whispering, "I'll be back in a few weeks, Pop. I love you."

Fernandez felt tears prickle his eyelids. He hadn't gone back in a few weeks.

And his father was right: "Living alone sucks."

...27

MONDAY MORNING the weather was seasonably warm. Fernandez crossed Melody Lane and found a bench facing the river, one without bird droppings. As he watched the gulls bobbing tranquilly on the rising tide, he noticed Avram Markus enter the market. Markus was not an imposing man, physically. He was gaunt, and with the help of his odd-looking cane, he walked with a bit of a stoop and a shuffle. Markus strolled along the water's edge, his eyes locked on Fernandez. His neighbor smiled, waved and continued on toward the library.

Markus was an enigma. He was gracious and friendly, but there was something in the man's ice-cold blue eyes that made Fernandez feel uneasy. As he started leafing through the *New York Times,* one news item attracted his attention.

> LONDON—Britain's counterterrorism police on Tuesday took over the investigation involving Vladimir Kara-Murza 35, a prominent Kremlin critic and Russian opposition figure who has been in a coma for over a week. Kara-Murza has been diagnosed with "acute poisoning by an undefined substance."
>
> Kara-Murza is not the first Putin critic to have been poisoned. Former Russian spy Alexander Litvinenko died in London in 2006 after drinking tea found to be laced with polonium-210, a radioactive substance. An inquiry last year concluded two Russian agents murdered Litvinenko and that the hit was "probably approved" by Putin.

Fernandez finished reading the *New York Times* article. He stared at the Indian River Bridge, then took a breath and squeezed his eyes shut for a second, remembering that eventful day.

After killing William Glenner, he had returned to Fort Pierce. The next morning he'd loaded his attache case with large stones and walked to the highest point on the bridge. There he'd checked to see if the used American Airlines ticket to the Virgin Islands was inside, along with his forged passport and black-finished compact Glock .357. He'd locked the case and dropped it over the bridge, where it sank to the deepest part of the Indian River.

He was startled when Ben Herman tapped him on the shoulder. "Another dead body, I hear." Herman grinned. "I suppose in your line of endeavor, that's good for business."

According to Fernandez's calculations, Ben Herman was over sixty years old. Life had left its mark on the semi-retired newspaperman. *The New York Times* article lay open on the bench.

Herman glanced at the newspaper article, and his brow furrowed. "Fucking Russians. The guy was injected with poison; nothing new about that. I've seen it before."

"What do you mean 'nothing new'?"

"You were FBI. You should know."

"Word never filtered down to the trenches. Tell me."

"It happened when I was working for the *Baltimore Sun*, before the buyout, when the bastards cut me loose."

Fernandez waited for Herman to continue.

"A few days before Christmas, the President went on TV and shocked the nation with news that his vice president, C.J. Landry, was dead. According to the President,

Landry suffered a heart attack while attending a Christmas party at a Washington homeless shelter hospital."

Fernandez remembered Quint Langstaff discussing Landry's death.

Herman touched his nose. "Something didn't smell right to me. I dug deep and found Landry and CIA Director Dorothy Schreck were colluding with Saudi Arabia to foment a war between Israel and Iran."

"Jesus."

"There's more. A source close to the investigation told me off-the-record that the last person Landry spoke with before his so-called heart attack was an old guy with a cane. Before I could get more information, the White House cracked down on leakers—my sources went all jittery. The administration didn't want to embarrass the Saudis and jeopardize oil imports."

"Do you think Landry was assassinated?"

Herman gave a wintry grin. "Injected with a poison."

"Who was responsible?"

"The mystery man with a cane, I suppose."

"Interesting."

"Why the interest? My news nose is twitching."

Something told Fernandez to leave that subject alone. He shook his head.

"Come on," Herman prodded. "Tell Uncle Ben."

"Got nothing for you, pal—sorry."

"I think you're full of shit, Fernandez." Herman got up and stalked off. It wasn't a pleasant parting.

Fernandez looked out at the Indian River. The seagulls were gone. Farther out, pelicans cruised, then folded their wings and dropped like stones.

Ben Herman had corroborated Langstaff's information: an old man with a cane had assassinated the vice president of the United States. He tried unsuccessfully to push the conversation with Ben Herman out of his mind and not engage in wild conspiracy theories. The other night, when he'd asked Markus about his career, Markus had related that he'd worked for an exterminator firm.

Fernandez couldn't picture Avram chasing termites; not a man who was familiar with anti-surveillance protocols and planted tape across his doorstep.

Enough, Fernandez told his tired, hyperactive imagination. *Enough.*

* * *

FERNANDEZ WAS IN NEED OF advice and lunch. He knew where both could be found. At the Seaway Drive train crossing, he stopped his car as the warning light flashed red. He listened to the *c-clack, c-clack, c-clack* sound of the northbound freight rattling by. After the train cleared the crossing, Fernandez heard the bell ring, and the gates rose to their fully upright position. The sound of the rattling train reminded him of something, but he couldn't put his finger on it.

* * *

SEOUL GARDENS WAS LOCATED on the southeast side of U.S. Route 1 at Virginia Avenue. The restaurant was busy. Mrs. Kym, the owner, greeted Fernandez with a warm smile. She was a short woman with white hair and a kind but worn face.

A year earlier, Fernandez had investigated the murder of a Korean War veteran, Earle Mayfield, the man who had occupied the apartment Avram Markus now rented. In the course of the investigation, Myung Kym and her grandson, Ji-hoon, had been considered people of interest by the police, until Fernandez had uncovered the real murderer.

In 1951, Mrs. Kym's parents had been killed in an atrocity committed by American soldiers under the command of Mayfield. Over the years, the Pentagon denied allegations that U.S. soldiers had perpetuated a massacre of South Korean civilians at the Pukhan River. However, eight-year-old Myung Kym was an eyewitness and survivor of the grim tragedy.

The murdered veteran, Mayfield, was a regular patron of Seoul Gardens. A conversation overheard by a waiter between Mayfield and two fellow veterans revealed Mayfield's first-hand knowledge of the Pukhan River tragedy.

Mrs. Kym's grandson, Ji-hoon, was in the kitchen at the time. He was told the story. The kid was a computer whiz. Ji-hoon was disturbed by what the waiter had overheard. He hacked into the Pentagon's main database and extracted Mayfield's military documents.

The Pentagon had thought their computer systems were hack-proof, when out of the blue, someone had penetrated top-secret files. The President was furious that the Pentagon's system had been breached, considering the money invested in consultants and security measures.

The government tracked the computer intrusion to an Indian River College computer and finally to Ji-hoon Kym. The Secretary of Defense said, "Go find the son-of-a-bitch and hire him before WikiLeaks gets him."

Currently, Ji-hoon Kym had a high paying job in Washington and Fernandez enjoyed free *kimchi,* the restaurant's signature dish.

Myung Kym sat in the booth beside Fernandez. She stared at him. The skin knotted around her eyes.

"What is trouble, Mister Frank?"

Fernandez was working a hunch. He handed her a handwritten note. "I need a favor from your grandson."

Mrs. Kym's eyes widened slightly. She nodded.

"Some years ago, a man assassinated the vice president of the United States and killed another high official. I believe I know the identity of the person who committed the crimes. He's old now. But I feel guilty remaining silent. After all you have been through, what do you think I should do?"

Fernandez caught the sadness in her eyes.

"You in large danger, Mr. Frank?"

"I don't think so."

"Is big reward?"

"No."

Myung Kym fell silent for a moment.

"In Korea, we have saying: 'Fish no get in trouble if it keep mouth shut.'"

Fernandez had to laugh. "Sounds like good advice."

"I fix you *kimchi.*" Myung Kym bowed her head and disappeared into the kitchen.

Fernandez's mind wandered to Garcella Beauvoir. He could understand that his barroom spat with Emerson had infuriated the discipline-oriented police chief. But what didn't compute was why she was dismissive of his help, with two unresolved murders on her plate and no suspects.

When his lunch arrived, Fernandez tasted the spicy, sour cabbage dish and slow-sipped a small glass of *sake*. He heard a train whistle in the distance. The *c-clack, c-clack* of the railroad crossing reminded him of Garcella's stuttering. He wondered what caused stuttering and decided to ask his brother.

"Sorry to bother you, Martin. I need your help."

He heard his brother inhale. "Your heart?"

"No. It's connected to the murder case I'm working. What can you tell me about speech defects? What causes a person to stammer?"

Martin sounded irritated. "Look it up on Google."

"Please. It could be important."

"It's not my field, but I'll give you the short version: speech defects can be genetic or occur from head injuries or emotional trauma—like child abuse. If you need more, I can recommend a neurologist."

"Thanks, Martin. Sorry to bother you."

"Hold on a sec," his brother said. "I did have an experience along those lines some years ago. I was working in the Hopkins emergency room. A girl about thirteen was brought in. Her name was Charlotte—as I recall. Charlotte was crossing Eastern Avenue with her mother when a drunk driver ran a light. He didn't see them. The girl pushed her mother out of the way—saving her life. Charlotte was struck head-on." Martin paused. "There was nothing I could do."

When Fernandez remained silent, his brother added, "Charlotte's father was suffering from a chronic motor tic condition and a speech disorder. Crazy as it sounds, after Charlotte's tragic death, her father lost his tic and his stammer. I believe emotional shocks can have physical manifestations."

Before he rang off, Martin Fernandez attempted to lighten the mood with a lame Porky Pig imitation: "Well, th-th-that's all, folks," he said.

I'm not sure that's all, Fernandez thought.

He recalled their last conversation. "Emerson's been suspended," Garcella had said. "He's off the force. And your presence is also no longer welcome." Fernandez heaved a deep sigh. For whatever reason, Garcella had lost her stammer.

After finishing his lunch, he tried to pay the check. Mrs. Kym pushed his hand away. He leaned over and hugged the old woman.

Myung Kym whispered, "I speak grandson. Is okay."

Fernandez was working a hunch. On a napkin, he scribbled a note.

"Another favor, please."

…28

BY FOUR P.M. FERNANDEZ HAD ARRIVED back at his apartment. At his front door was a package containing the paperback he'd ordered: *The Fine Art of Provenance,* by Justin Williams. He leafed through Williams' book. The dedication was simple:

FOR HW
1954—1963

Fernandez read for a while until his eyes became tired. The book explained how sales of valuable artwork should be accompanied by documentation, known as provenance, to confirm authenticity. But what Fernandez had been searching for were insights into Justin Williams' personal life.

The book dedication was intriguing. He wondered if the short-lived individual with initials HW had been a relative. This thought drew him back to Justin Williams' black address book.

Thumbing through, he found a telephone number for an Arthur Williams with a 575 area code. A quick check on Google revealed 575 was a Taos, New Mexico area code. Fernandez checked his watch. Taos was one hour behind. He rang up the number. A woman's voice answered.

"Arthur Williams, please."

"Is this a sales call?"

"No, ma'am. I'm calling about a matter concerning a Mr. Justin Williams."

"Not again!" she blurted.

Fernandez heard a muffled conversation.

"This is Arthur Williams."

"Sir, are you a relative of Justin Williams?"

"I'm his brother. What's going on?"

"My name is Fernandez. I'm an investigator assisting the Fort Pierce Police Department—"

"What do you want?"

"I'm sorry to tell you … your brother, Justin, is dead."

The line went quiet.

"Are you still there, Mr. Williams?"

"How did Justin die?"

"Shot to death by an intruder."

Fernandez heard a stifled sob.

"Do you know someone with the initials HW?"

"That would be Helene, our sister. Justin loved her dearly. Helene died at age nine. Under the weight of the poor girl's sickness and death, I think my brother's psychological space suffered a severe warp. He developed an unhealthy attitude toward young girls. Maybe it was their childlike virginal quality, reminiscent of his sister."

"Are you saying your brother was a … pedophile?"

"More like … mentally ill," Williams snapped. "I talked with specialists. There was something occurring in his brain that caused Justin to be sexually attracted towards something he shouldn't have been. They recommended therapy and medications to help him manage *those* feelings … and not to act on them."

"What did your parents do?"

"Nothing. Denial. When Justin was twenty-one, he left and went to New York." Arthur sighed again. "My brother became a published author and a museum administrator, but he refused to seek professional help. Eventually, I gave up trying and had to sever all contact."

"The lady who answered the phone said, 'Not again.' What did she mean?"

"This is not the first time my brother was investigated, but he was never charged with a crime. Justin wasn't evil; he was sick and wouldn't seek help."

Fernandez kept his opinion in check.

"Was there a funeral?"

"Justin Williams was cremated."

"Just as well. After his ashes are scattered, this whole thing will be put to rest."

Not for the victims, Fernandez thought.

...29

TWO EMPTY BOTTLES OF WINE stood sentinel on the table next to him. Fernandez had fallen asleep in his recliner in front of the television. It was late morning when he climbed out of the leather chair with a headache, a protesting back and a full bladder.

From the bathroom, he shuffled to the kitchen for coffee and then the front door for the newspaper. As Fernandez reached for the paper, he found a plain, unaddressed envelope, inside of which was a computer printout and a handwritten note.

Dear Mr. F:
Found Garcella Beauvoir in Boston police files.
Avram Markus in CIA Files: code-name SCORPION.
Access denied.
Sorry.

"Code-name Scorpion," Fernandez murmured. He had suspected Markus worked for a government agency.

Ji-hoon Kym's report on Garcella Beauvoir was comprehensive. Fernandez sat at his desk and skimmed the printout.

Garcella Beauvoir, born 1963, Providence, R.I. Mother, Bessie Beauvoir worked as housekeeper. Father's identity unknown. 1976 Beauvoir awarded art scholarship to Rhode Island School of Design. In 1978, at age 14, Garcella surprised her sponsors by quitting Rhode Island

School of Design. She went to live with grandmother in Boston.

1982, Garcella Beauvoir received tuition-paid college scholarship. She graduated with a criminal justice degree from Bridgewater State University in Bridgewater, Massachusetts.

1986, Beauvoir joined Boston Police Department as a police officer. 1990, received promotion to sergeant, and lieutenant in 1994.

According to sources, Beauvoir's speech impediment limited promotional opportunities.

1998, Beauvoir accepted job as Chief of Police, Edgartown, Mass. Seven years later she was recruited to head Portland, Maine Police Department. She served in that capacity until moving to Florida.

Fernandez read the report a second time and then flicked through the papers in his desk drawer until he found Williams' file. From 1976 to 1978 Justin Williams had been an instructor at the school Garcella had attended when she was fourteen years old. Both individuals had been at the same school at the same time?

He pressed his hands against his eyes and drew a deep breath. *Dig deep enough into a case, you find links.* The disconnected dots slid into place. Justin Williams had sexually molested Garcella while she was attending art school in Rhode Island. It had taken Garcella Beauvoir a long time, but with a coldness that implied planning and intent, she had exacted her revenge.

His throat felt dry as he searched for loopholes in his theory—and how to prove it.

Fernandez turned on his computer and waited for it to boot up. He Googled the Portland, Maine Police Department, and then with his iPhone, he tapped in their number.

A female voice answered. "Police department. How can we help you?"

He cleared his throat. "Garcella Beauvoir, please."

"Captain Beauvoir no longer works here."

"I'm with a recruiting company. We have a lucrative opening on the Minneapolis Police force."

"Garcella moved to Florida. She was tired of cold weather. Can't say as I much blame her."

"Why did Captain Beauvoir pick a small town like Fort Pierce?"

"You're asking a lot of questions, mister."

"Sorry to bother you, ma'am. Have a blessed day."

Fernandez disconnected. He glanced at Justin Williams' file and found the number for another museum, the Joslyn Art Museum. He was connected to Melvin Wyman, the man in charge.

"Sir, my name is Fernandez, from Fort Pierce, Florida. I am investigating the murder of a man named Justin Williams. He was connected with your museum from 1979 to 1983."

"Oh my," Wyman said.

"Did you know Mr. Williams?"

Wyman offered nothing in response.

"Can you hear me, sir?"

"Yes. I heard you. Williams was my predecessor. I hardly knew the man."

"Why did Mr. Williams leave Joslyn Art Museum and move to Canada?"

"I'm sure I have no idea."

Fernandez knew the man was lying. "Mr. Wyman, we could subpoena you to come to Fort Pierce and testify under oath."

He heard Wyman pause and inhale deeply. "Well, I heard rumors … some parents complained of … inappropriate behavior."

"Was Justin Williams suspected of sexual abuse? Is that why he left the country?"

There was silence on the line.

"Mr. Wyman—"

"If you have further inquiries," Wyman said, "please contact our attorneys."

The man hung up.

Fernandez looked at his notes and called the Arkansas Art Center in Little Rock, Arkansas. After explaining that he was working on a murder investigation of a former employee, he was connected to the executive director, Roger Dalsheimer.

"I'm investigating the murder of a man named Justin Williams," Fernandez said.

"Justin Williams is dead?"

"Yes, sir."

"I'm delighted to have received the news. Goodbye."

Fernandez made another phone call. The Portland, Maine mayor explained that he had never understood why Garcella had turned down excellent offers from the Baltimore and Philadelphia police departments.

Things were coming together: the golden triangle of any criminal investigation. Motive, means and opportunity.

He turned his theory around and around: it seemed rational. Garcella Beauvoir had motive: revenge on the sexual predator who had soiled her and altered her life course.

She was a police officer with access to a weapon, possibly one that was unregistered. Justin Williams would have recognized Garcella and welcomed her into his home.

If any traces of hair or fingerprints had been left after Williams was shot, they would be ignored, because as officer-in-charge, Garcella was on the crime scene before they dusted for prints. She had contrived to keep Fernandez distanced from the crime scene and off the case. In a perverse way, it was a compliment.

Fernandez slowly rose from his desk chair and made his way to his bedroom to shower and decide how to handle the situation. If he was still with the FBI or employed by the police department, he could request a judge to authorize a search warrant for Garcella's residence to try and locate the murder weapon.

As a private investigator, Fernandez had no legal standing to request a warrant. He reviewed the people who might help: Lou Brumberg was retired; Miriam Jolson, as medical examiner, was out of the loop; Floyd Emerson was on temporary suspension, but under the circumstances, legally eligible. He felt uneasy contacting Emerson. At their last encounter, Emerson had called Charlie a bastard and Fernandez had decked him.

He shrugged and tapped in Emerson's number.

Floyd Emerson must have seen Fernandez' name on the screen. "What do you want?"

"Listen. I'm sorry for losing my cool and hitting you. It was just a tense situation, you know?"

"I'm a detective, Fernandez. Remember? You didn't call me to apologize. So what the hell do you want?"

Fernandez took a deep breath. "I need your help, Floyd. There's serious shit going down in the police department.

You would be the last person I would call under other circumstances."

Emerson didn't respond.

Fernandez knew, at heart, the guy was decent and a solid detective. Sometimes alcohol and a messy home situation made Emerson act like an asshole.

"I'm curious," Emerson said. "What's the deal?"

"Come to my apartment ASAP. I'll explain everything. Just hear me out, Floyd. If you're not interested, go play golf."

Emerson grumbled, "Fuck," and disconnected.

Fernandez wasn't certain whether that was yes or no.

* * *

FIFTEEN MINUTES LATER FERNANDEZ heard a knock at his door.

"That was fast."

"Fort Pierce is a small town."

"Sit down, Floyd, and hear me out."

Fernandez explained everything: the connection of Garcella with Williams at the Rhode Island School of Design; Garcella's departure from the school and from her art career; evidence of Justin Williams' suspected pedophilia at the Joslyn Art Museum in Nebraska.

He mentioned that since Williams' death, Garcella no longer stammered. He traced her police career and how she'd kept track of Williams. When the job opening occurred, she'd turned down more lucrative opportunities to come to Fort Pierce.

Emerson looked gut-punched as Fernandez outlined his theory. "You got to give her credit," he said, shaking his head. "After what that poor girl went through, she had the stones to put her life back together, build a career and reach the rank of police captain. Damn."

Fernandez nodded, letting Emerson process the information.

Emerson took out his cell phone and cancelled his golf match. "What do you have in mind?" he asked.

"I have no official standing. Everything is circumstantial evidence. As of now, no actual proof."

"Where do I come in?"

"We need the murder weapon. That requires a search warrant for Garcella's apartment. You're a member of the police department. You can make that happen."

Emerson snapped his fingers. "Judge Pines," he said. "Let me pull up a search warrant requisition and see if I can catch him at the courthouse. I'll get back to you."

After Emerson left, Fernandez could do nothing but wait. Ji-hoon Kym's report had opened investigative floodgates. He had rushed in like a trained bloodhound, following the scent to where it led. He knew no other way; it was his ingrained FBI training.

Now Fernandez was feeling conflicted and a little remorseful. Garcella Beauvoir had suffered unacceptable sexual mistreatment and had taken, at least in his mind, understandable revenge on her abuser.

Fernandez recognized his hypocrisy in accusing her of doing exactly what he had done years before, enacting revenge on the man who had betrayed him. He considered slowing down the investigation, taking time to rethink the situation.

His cell phone buzzed. It was Floyd Emerson.

"We're good to go."

...30

"GARCELLA," FERNANDEZ SAID. "The Riverside Art Museum retained me to investigate the murder of Justin Williams."

"Good for you."

He cleared his throat. "It's imperative we talk. Can you meet me in your office?"

"I'm sorry, Frank. Tuesday is my day off. I'm going to visit my mother in her memory care facility in Vero Beach. She doesn't know who she is anymore. The good news is, she meets new people every day. Including me."

"I *know* who murdered Justin Williams. Meet me in an hour—your office." He disconnected the call before she could respond.

Fernandez telephoned Lisa Rodriguez. "Lisa, do you still clean Captain Garcella Beauvoir's apartment in Renaissance on the River?"

"Yes, sir."

"You have a key to her unit?"

"I do."

*   *   *

THE POLICE CHIEF LOOKED UP when Fernandez entered her office. Her glasses slipped slightly. She peered at him over the black frames. Their eyes met for a brief moment, and there was a thick silence in the room.

A furrow appeared between her eyes. "Okay. What's so important?"

"I notice that you no longer stammer."

"How perceptive. I have a speech therapist. Would you like her name?"

Fernandez pressed ahead. "As I said on the phone, I know who killed Justin Williams."

Her face was expressionless. Fernandez had been hoping for a tell—some sort of a sign that he had been on the right track.

"Do you?" Garcella said. "Please enlighten me."

"In 1976, a talented young art student attended the Rhode Island Institute of Design. While she was there, she was sexually abused by a professor."

Her countenance was stone.

"This art professor was a pedophile. He moved on to other museums in other cities. The museums, like some churches seeking to avoid unfavorable publicity, failed to report claims of child abuse."

Garcella held his gaze, unblinking.

"The girl developed a speech defect as a result of the trauma she had experienced. She gave up art, quit school and went to live with her grandmother in Boston. Rather than pursue an art career, the bright young woman chose criminal justice. She joined the Boston police department and rose through the ranks, eventually ending up as police chief in Portland, Maine.

"In my conversation with Portland Mayor Chester Dawson, he said his police chief was offered the top job in the Baltimore and Philadelphia police departments, but chose Fort Pierce for reasons he could never understand. With me so far?"

She smiled distantly.

"Everybody makes mistakes," Fernandez said, feeling like a hypocritical prick. "Our luck runs out—"

Garcella scoffed audibly. "You have a well-earned reputation for constructing unprovable theories—like fingering McCuskey for Leroy Martin's murder. In real-life police work, we require evidence. Have you any hard evidence for this fairy tale?"

"Not yet."

"You need a career change, Fernandez. With your imagination, take up fiction writing. And now if you'll excuse me, I need to go see my mother."

As Garcella started to rise from her desk, they heard a knock on her door. Floyd Emerson entered.

"Reality check," Emerson said. "Found nothing."

Garcella Beauvoir slumped back in her seat. Her voice was a whisper, a sigh. "Were you planning to ask your suspect if she could provide an alibi for her whereabouts the night of Williams' murder?"

Fernandez was struck silent with her audacity.

Emerson was the first to respond. "We're listening."

Garcella formed a gun with her thumb and finger and pointed it at the men. "You are both dumber than a sack of rocks. At the time of the murder, I was in bed with an unimpeachable witness—Miriam Jolson.

"As for Justin Williams, he was my worst nightmare, but I got over it. In fact, until he was reported murdered, I didn't know the son-of-a-bitch was still alive."

Garcella gave an amiable nod. "So let's move on to your next bad theory."

...31

"GOOD NEWS," MARIS SAID when she phoned. "The Riverside Museum wants me to interview for the director's job. I have a meeting set for tomorrow afternoon. I thought Charlie and I would drive over tonight ... and stay with you."

"Love it. Just give me time to clean up after last night's party and throw away the empty whiskey bottles and used condoms—"

"In your dreams, sugar."

Maris arrived in Fort Pierce just after dark. They hugged briefly, efficiently. Fernandez leaned into the back and gently lifted Charlie from the car seat, supporting his weight with one arm. The boy instinctively threw his arms around Fernandez's neck, his face slack from slumber.

"I think he's ready for bed," Maris said.

Charlie looked up, squinted, and then nodded off again.

When they were settled in the living room drinking wine, Fernandez said, "How did it go with the doctor?"

Maris hesitated before answering. "Some children reach the age of three without being able to say a single word. Picasso could draw before he could talk, and Einstein was four or five before he spoke; they thought he was retarded."

"We're not discussing Picasso or Einstein. We're discussing Charlie."

"Charlie understands what's going on, you know. He just doesn't communicate verbally—a word here, a word there. It's not a hearing issue or intelligence issue. He loves to sit and play games on the computer and draw pictures."

"What did the doctor say?"

"They gave Charlie a complete physical and neurological examination as well as a psychological evaluation to determine his intelligence level, and ... the psychiatrist said, 'Just give him time.' So I'm not pressing."

She changed the subject. "I'm a little nervous about the museum interview tomorrow. Did they find out who killed Justin Williams?"

Fernandez involuntarily shook his head. "No."

Maris added, "I'm sure the museum is delighted to have the Picasso painting. It's bound to drive up attendance."

"Justin Williams thought *Boy with a Pipe* was overrated," Fernandez said. "Not worth a hundred million—"

Maris pursed her lips. "A painting, like a house, is worth what the market is willing to pay for it. No more, no less."

"When I showed *Boy with a Pipe* to Captain Beauvoir, it really upset her. She told me Picasso was both a creator of art and a destroyer of women."

"Are you finished, dear?"

"I also found that Picasso was greedy and left an estate worth fifty million."

Maris laughed. "When you let an over-the-hill investigator loose in the art world, you never know what he'll turn up with." She paused. "Isn't it passing strange that a police captain was rattled over abusive behavior? In her line of work, wouldn't she be accustomed to dealing with violence against women?"

Fernandez wasn't listening. He could feel an erection begin to throb against the inside of his pants. "It's been a long time," he remarked with a sigh.

"Not tonight," Maris said gently, touching his cheek. "I'm worn out, and I have to prepare for the interview. Maybe another time." She went to sleep on the sofa.

Fernandez felt resentful. What he didn't know was that the next day would be the worst day of his life.

PART VIII

THE OLIGARCH

"Пожалéл волк кобы́лу, остáвил хвост да гри́ву."

"The wolf spared the little mare;
it left a tail and a mane."
—Russian proverb

...32

WEDNESDAY MORNING Fernandez was awakened by a phone call. A voice in broken English said, "You name Fernandez?"

"That's right, who are—"

"Grisha Chuychenko. Where my painting is?"

"If you are referring to Picasso's *Boy with a Pipe*, the painting has been transferred to the Riverside Art Museum in Vero Beach. You will need to talk to Mrs. Gilman—"

"Bullshit you speak. I pay one hundred five million—Sotheby's deliver me a fake."

"I'm sorry. It's out of my hands."

Fernandez heard the Russian ask a question, and someone muttered something in response. Chuychenko came back on the line. "My boat is come Fort Pierce."

"I don't have the painting."

"You have little boy. You want keep boy safe, eh?"

"Don't threaten me. I'm an ex-FBI agent and I can—"

The Russian cut him off. "We have Russian proverb. "*Пожале́л волк кобы́лу, оста́вил хвост да гри́ву*. The wolf spared the little mare; it left a tail and a mane."

"Hold on, goddamnit."

"If you want boy live, you get painting, say nothing. Understand?"

Chuychenko disconnected.

A shiver ran through Fernandez. He felt paralyzed by the Russian's threat. He had to force himself to breathe deeply and think. What to do? Whom to call?

Contacting the Bureau was out of the question. In kidnapping cases, he knew FBI agents didn't face disciplinary actions if victims got killed. That was sometimes viewed as unavoidable collateral damage. Agents only suffered career consequences if the kidnappers got away.

The Russian's parting words haunted him. "The wolf spared the little mare; it left a tail and a mane."

Fernandez knew he only had a few hours to prepare. He called Brumberg.

"Lou, I need help. Your godson is in danger. I received a kidnapping threat. Please send a couple of ex-SEALs to take Maris and Charlie from my apartment to your place until this mess is over."

"No problem."

"And assign some SEALs to guard your unit around the clock. Send me the bill."

"I'm on it."

Next he woke Maris.

"Honey, I know it's early. We have a problem."

"I don't like the way you said that."

"Some SEALs are taking you to Brumberg's place in Ocean Village."

"What are you involved in?" Maris raged. "I warned you—"

"A Russian oligarch thinks I have the Picasso. He's making crazy threats. I need you and Charlie safe."

"Now hold on just a goddamn minute, Frank."

"Gotta run. Bye."

Fernandez had another person to contact. He didn't want to. He had no choice.

* * *

AVRAM MARKUS DIDN'T BLINK when Fernandez explained the situation. He absorbed the Russian's conversation without comment. Then his heavy, sad face lifted slightly in a small smile.

"You needn't worry too much. We are dealing with a rich *apparatchik*. A former KGB operative would have taken your boy first and then contacted you."

Markus put his hand on Fernandez's shoulder. "Stay calm. I still have a few contacts, if they're not dead from cirrhosis or old age."

Avram ambled into the bedroom, returning with an odd-looking cell phone and a faded address book bound with thick rubber bands. He checked his watch. "Seven hours' difference." Then he punched in a number.

Fernandez heard a voice answer "*Da*."

"I need to talk to Viktor Chirkov. Is the old Cossack still alive?"

"Who wants to know?" a raspy voice demanded.

"Tell Viktor it's the Scorpion, *Zasranec*, asshole."

Markus held up his cell phone. "Untraceable. The activation number puts me in touch with an operator working a call center in India. I tell them the IMEI number, and I have a working phone. After forty-eight hours, the number is erased until a new one is reactivated."

While they waited, Fernandez said, "I heard you say you were the Scorpion."

Markus waved a hand dismissively. "Years ago, I worked for your CIA—with some distinction, I might add. Things changed. The Agency became politicized. Our parting was not amiable. The CIA does not wish me well … and the feeling is mutual."

A low and quiet voice came on the line.

"Avram, old friend, good to hear from you."

"How is it going, Viktor?"

"Even in ashes there are yet a few sparks."

"You old rascal."

"Better a rascal than a fool," Viktor Chirkov said. "And why, I ask myself, after all these years, do I merit a call? Then I remembered, we are in your debt for—"

Avram broke in. "That was a personal matter."

Markus excused himself and continued the call in the bedroom. Fernandez couldn't hear what was being said.

* * *

"NOW WE PROCEED," Avram said, returning to the living room. He tapped in Grisha Chuychenko's private number and waited while it rang.

"*Zdrahstvooytee,*" a gruff voice said.

"Do I have the pleasure of addressing Mr. Grisha Chuychenko?"

"Who is this? How you get private number?"

Avram winked at Fernandez. "My name is Morris, sir. Adrian Morris. I deal in valuable artwork. It is my business to know how to contact major art collectors—with special offers."

"Talk, I listen."

"I have in my possession a Chagall oil on canvas painted in 1913. This valuable painting is one of Chagall's Fiddler series, a violinist in a rustic Russian village."

"Much fake shit floating around. What kind provenance you got?"

"I have the original bill of sale and a certificate of authenticity from the Freemanart Consultancy Forensic

Laboratory in North America. You are invited to contact them. Further, if we reach accord, your own experts will have the opportunity to use high resolution scans or infrared spectrometry to examine the painting."

"Why you not sell through auction house?"

"My clients prefer confidential transactions. Even with anonymous buyers at auctions, word gets out. I contacted you, Mr. Chuychenko, because of your esteemed reputation in the art world. If you have no interest, I am sorry to have troubled you."

"If I have interest, how much?"

"The asking price is 4.18 million dollars."

"Is negotiable?"

"Everything in life is negotiable."

"Where you are?"

"Palm Beach, Florida."

"You come my boat, *Putinesca.* Fort Pierce Marina, three o'clock. Bring painting—we talk. Is okay?"

"I would like to oblige you, sir, but as I am in possession of a valuable work of art, it is protocol that our first meeting be arranged at a neutral location. There is a library in Fort Pierce a short distance from the marina. My associate will meet you at the entrance at, shall we say, three thirty?"

The Russian's tone turned argumentative and insulting. "You not trust me?"

When Avram spoke again he sounded tired, as though the Russian's angry comment had worn him down. He spoke quietly.

"With all due respect, sir, I will be at the Fort Pierce library at the time specified. If you are not present, I will sell the Chagall to one of my clients in Palm Beach."

"*Zakolebal*. I come."

"What did he say?" Fernandez asked.

"He said that I pissed him off."

"How can you show the Russian a fake Chagall?"

"For this meeting, what I have will suffice."

Markus pushed his chair back and stood up. "Meet me at the library at two o'clock. Wear a suit and tie. Do you have a weapon?"

"Yes, a .357 Smith & Wesson."

"Shoulder holster?"

Fernandez nodded.

"Chuychenko will not come alone. They must see you are armed."

"What if the Russian saw my photo in the newspaper and asks about the Picasso?"

"Tell him everything will be resolved."

Avram gripped Fernandez's shoulder, "After you greet Chuychenko, direct him to the second-floor meeting room and then immediately leave the area."

"How will I know when my family is safe?"

"You will know. Trust me. You will know."

...33

THE GLEAMING ORANGE AND YELLOW clay tiles on the Fort Pierce Library roof sparkled in the tropical sun. A gentle breeze blew in from the river.

The Russian oligarch's two sullen bodyguards looked like professional wrestlers stuffed into black business suits, tight at the shoulders. The first man loitered near a jacaranda tree on Melody Lane opposite the library. Under his jacket was the bulge of a gun. He stared openly at Fernandez. His partner leaned against a car in the parking area with his arms crossed.

Fernandez saw Chuychenko's yacht anchored at the marina. The vessel had three decks with wraparound windows and twin jet skis docked on the stern.

The bodyguard at the jacaranda tree gave a nod. A man with a shaved head and gleaming skull approached Fernandez at the library entrance. Chuychenko was dressed in dark pants and a black cashmere turtleneck sweater.

Neither man spoke in the elevator. At the second-floor landing, Fernandez directed the Russian to the meeting room in the corridor on the right. He left after he heard Avram speaking Russian. "*Kahk pahzhivaheetyeh*?"

Fernandez ignored the bodyguards, who stood on the pavement looking as useful as potted plants. He walked the few blocks to his condominium parking lot. He was so deep in thought that he was only jerked out of his reverie by noticing his left rear tire was flat. Impossible. He had just purchased four new tires.

He felt his heart fibrillate. His lips went dry. The Miami warehouse ambush flashed through his mind. He didn't know whether he was being cautious or paranoid. Fernandez stood very still and listened. There was no sound. Even the light breeze off the river had died. The parking lot was completely deserted. He edged into the shadows of the building.

Protecting his family was the first priority. He made his way cautiously to the Seaway Smokehouse Restaurant located next door and phoned for a cab. While he waited, he recalled an FBI briefing about a well-known Mafia killer called the Iceman who specialized in parking lot assaults. He would park close to a mark's car, give it a flat, then return to his van. When the mark returned, spotted the flat, and opened his trunk to bend over and pull out the spare tire, the Iceman would steal up behind him and put a .38 in his lower back. After that, he would handcuff him, tape his mouth shut, and drive to a predetermined location to shoot the mark in the back of the head twice, then dispose of the body.

Fernandez wondered if the Mafia hitman was still alive. He tapped in "Iceman" on his iPhone.

> The Iceman—Richard Kuklinski (April 11, 1935 – March 5, 2006) Serial killer and mob hitman associated with DeCavalcante crime family of Newark, New Jersey. Kuklinski was named "The Iceman" for freezing his victims to mask time of death.

* * *

IT WAS FOUR P.M. when Fernandez's cab arrived.

"Sorry, sir," the driver said. "Traffic downtown was snarled up. Something going on at the marina."

At Lou Brumberg's apartment, Maris opened the door.

He held both hands up. "I'm sorry. Please give me a chance to explain."

Maris made a poor job of masking her resentment.

"Hey, Frank," Brumberg yelled. "Listen to this."

Fernandez grabbed the TV remote and increased the volume. On CNN the anchorwoman breathlessly announced, "Late breaking news from Fort Pierce, Florida. Grisha Chuychenko, a Russian businessman and confidant of Russian President Vladimir Putin, was taken by ambulance to Lawnwood Regional Medical Center, where the Russian oligarch was pronounced dead upon arrival.

"Mark Winslow, captain of Chuychenko's yacht, told police his employers had come to Fort Pierce to negotiate the purchase of a Chagall painting and to regain possession of a valuable Picasso painting.

"According to sources close to the investigation, Grisha Chuychenko was invited to a private meeting at the local library to discuss the art purchase. Security men working for Chuychenko reported after the meeting they noticed their employer walking unsteadily and complaining of a pain in his right calf. When they rolled up his trouser leg, they noticed a small puncture wound.

"Grisha Chuychenko was helped back to his boat, where he collapsed and was transported by ambulance to the hospital. Rumors are circulating in Washington that the Russian oligarch's death was in retaliation for the recent poisoning of Vladimir Kara-Murza.

"Fort Pierce police chief Garcella Beauvoir said they were awaiting autopsy results. She requested the FBI to be involved in the case … and now a word from our sponsors. Stay tuned."

"Oh, shit! The FBI," Fernandez gulped. He realized he was an accessory to murder. The boat captain had overheard their conversation. Also, the librarian had recognized him and waved when Fernandez entered the building with Chuychenko.

He panicked. His apartment contained the hacked information, which could get Mrs. Kym's grandson fired or jailed.

"Lou, let me borrow your car."

He mumbled a half-hearted apology to Maris and headed for the door.

"Where do you think you're going?" Maris screamed.

"I have to go. Sorry."

"Don't you dare leave—"

Maris was talking to a closed door.

* * *

ARRIVING IN HIS APARTMENT, Fernandez emptied the bullets from his pistol. Then he shredded all notes, documents and paperwork related to Ji-hoon Kym and Avram Markus. As an extra precaution, he checked his computer and deleted any references to the two men.

After Fernandez had sanitized the apartment, he tried to contact Avram Markus. His phone was not in service. Fernandez rushed to his neighbor's unit and knocked repeatedly. Ethan Rogers, the building maintenance man, opened the door.

"I was just on my way to see you, Frank. Mr. Markus vacated his unit. He had to leave town—a family emergency. He told me to donate his furniture to the Haitian Church, and give this package to you in person."

* * *

FERNANDEZ UNWRAPPED THE BULKY five-by-six-foot package. Inside he was surprised to find Avram's Marc Chagall painting. With the painting was an envelope containing a letter and a folded, yellowed document.

My dear Frank,

Your son is safe. That is the most important thing.

Being a father is not just about love, it's about watching out for your children.

As a father myself, I experienced how cold and random the universe could be. I was in the Israeli Army and unable to protect my son, Zak, when his death came as an uninvited guest.

For personal and political reasons, I emigrated from Israel and joined the CIA. My past deeds cast a long shadow and as a result, I move around a lot.

In the blink of an eye, I had a son, and then just as quickly he was taken away. There are few emotional investments a man can make in his life like the one he makes in a son, whether that son carries his DNA or not.

We shall not see each other again. Remember me, Frank.

Kind regards,
Avram

P.S. Enclosed is the Fiddler *painting. It is the original, not a Chinese reproduction. Also enclosed is the provenance, Chagall's signed receipt.*

* * *

"MARIS LEFT," LOU BRUMBERG said. "I've known her since she was a pup. The only tears I ever seen that girl shed were over her father's flag-draped casket. You know her mother died of the big C. When I saw that little girl sitting all alone at Charlie's funeral, it was the saddest thing I can remember—and that includes 'Nam."

Fernandez felt a pang of guilt. "Lou, I had—"

"You don't need to explain nothing to me. You were in a bad situation, and I guess you did what you had to do. Nobody can be blamed for that."

"Thank you, Lou."

"I think you burned your bridges this time, Frank. Maris was more tearful than angry. She said, 'Uncle Lou. I can't live like this anymore. I will never sit by a flag-draped casket again.' Then she took little Charlie and headed back to St. Petersburg."

Fernandez was silent. He didn't have much else to say. He made an attempt to contact Maris on his landline. She was not accepting his calls. He put the phone gently back into its cradle and stared at it for a long time.

...34

HE KNEW THEY WOULD BE COMING. The Marc Chagall painting was too bulky to hide in his closet or under his bed. Fernandez followed Anthony Carlyle's example and hung the painting on the living room wall—in plain sight.

At nine a.m. Fernandez heard them knock. The two federal agents greeted Fernandez cordially, at first. The one in charge was tall, square-jawed, over forty-five, with hard, cold, gray eyes. The other was heavyset, his neck short and thickly muscled: a weight lifter.

"Mr. Fernandez," said Square Jaw, not bothering to shake hands. "I'm Agent Davis. This is my partner, Agent Collins." He sat in a chair without asking.

"What's this all about?" Fernandez asked as casually as he could.

"I know they called you Saint Fernandez in the good old days, because you were so pure of heart."

"Mr. Davis, don't patronize me," Fernandez said. "I appreciate your needling me to make me lose my cool. It's a good tactic. I've used it myself. I've got nothing to hide, so ask away."

"Good. I'll cut to the chase," said Davis, his tone steely. "The W. H. is in a stew over Chuychenko. They want answers, and they're leaning on the FBI. You know how the game is played when the President of the United States makes a phone call. So, tell us about your associate—what's his name?"

"Let's exchange information," Fernandez offered. "Tell me what you have, and I'll tell you what I know."

"That's bullshit," Collins sputtered. "Under terrorist threat authority, we can run your ass in and—"

Davis held up a restraining hand to his partner. "Frank's an alum. Let's give him a chance."

They're now playing good cop-bad cop, Fernandez thought. "Is the autopsy finished?" he asked.

Davis shook his head. "Not yet. We're waiting."

"I'll tell you what I know. I have a neighbor, Mr. Markus. Avram Markus."

Collins wrote it down.

"Friday morning, Mr. Markus knocked on my door. He was frightened. He had an appointment at the Fort Pierce library to sell artwork to a wealthy Russian. Mr. Markus was concerned about going alone carrying a valuable painting. He knew I had served in the FBI, and he asked me to go with him."

"According to eyewitness reports, you were armed."

"I'm legally licensed to carry a weapon in Florida. The weapon was unloaded. It was just for show."

"Where is Mr. Markus?"

"No idea."

Davis exhaled sharply. "You abetted Markus. You can be charged as an accomplice."

"You know better than that, Davis. I was helping a worried old man. I walked to the library, I saw Mr. Markus and his client were safely inside, and then I walked home. You can ask Chuychenko's two gorillas. They watched me leave."

"Then where did you go?"

"I went to Hutchinson Island to be with my family. They're visiting with former police chief Louis Brumberg."

"Convenient alibi. Now tell us about your *worried* neighbor."

Fernandez decided to share information but protect Jihoon Kym. "Mr. Markus rented in this building for a short time. On several occasions we had drinks together. One night after a little too much Metaxa brandy, Mr. Markus let slip he had connections with the CIA, code name: Scorpion."

"Right. Scorpion," Davis smirked. "You sure he wasn't the Green Hornet?"

Fernandez opened his palms. "That's all I know."

"Anything else you care to share?"

He sensed Davis was baiting a trap. "I had a personal problem with Chuychenko."

"The ship captain said Chuychenko threatened you?"

"The man was upset. I couldn't blame him. Years ago Chuychenko purchased a Picasso painting at auction for a ton of money. It turned out that the auction house sold him a forgery. I was hired to investigate a burglary after Hurricane Irma. One thing led to another, and we recovered the original Picasso painting."

"And Chuychenko was coming to Fort Pierce to retrieve it?" Davis said.

Fernandez nodded. "I told him I was out of the loop. He needed to talk to the Riverside Art Museum people."

"I've been around the block a few times," Davis said. "I think you're fucking with me, Fernandez."

The agent's phone chimed. He answered, then grimaced as he listened. "Are you certain?"

He disconnected. "Chuychenko's death was caused by lethal injection—scorpion venom."

The FBI man shook his head and exhaled slowly. "It must have been the CIA. Putin will have a shit fit."

* * *

AFTER THE FBI AGENTS LEFT, Fernandez tried to reach his wife again. The number rang several times and finally went to voice mail. He left a brief message asking Maris to call him and hung up. Then he called St. Lucie Tire and Battery.

"Your car is ready," the manager said.

"Did you find the problem?"

"The flat wasn't caused by a nail, screw or glass fragment, I can tell you that for sure. We don't get blowouts on our new tires. I think somebody shoved a sharp knife through the sidewall and slit your radial fibers—"

Fernandez interrupted. "I have a call coming in. Let me get back to you."

A well-modulated voice said, "I hope you will accept our warning, Mr. Fernandez. Drop the Williams case. My associates have a long reach, one that extends to the Virgin Islands and to an unsolved murder in Charlotte Amalie."

Before Fernandez could muster a reply, the caller added, "One hand washes the other … and as you know, there is no statute of limitation on murder."

* * *

FERNANDEZ FELT NUMB. If the Glenner murder in Charlotte Amalie was reopened or leaked to the press, his life was over. It was that simple. He forced himself to shower, dress and take a brisk walk, hoping to trigger some endorphins and be able to think clearly.

As he approached the Farmers' Market, Fernandez spotted Stanley Wilson, Grace Carlyle's maintenance man. Wilson was walking Bentley, the King Charles spaniel.

Wilson gave Fernandez a tight smile. "Fucking dog walker up and left." He shook his head. When Bentley started sniffing, Wilson sighed. "Can't have the damn dog shitting on the sidewalk. See you around."

Fernandez stopped to order coffee. As he opened his wallet to pay, a business card fell out. He stuffed the card in his pocket and sat at a small table, sipping coffee and trying to assess his predicament.

He didn't doubt the Mafia had connections in the Islands constabulary. Drug money bought a lot of friends. He replayed the conversation in his mind. The caller had used the phrasing "No statute of limitations on murder," the same threat he had used with DeCicco to solicit cooperation in the Leroy Martin investigation. Fernandez took out the business card DeCicco had given him.

SALVADORE COSTELLO
Attorney at Law
772-579-1000
By Appointment Only
4453 South U.S. 1 * Ft. Pierce, FL 34982

"Costello," Fernandez mused. Something stuck in his mind. Lori Costello was Grace Carlyle's dog walker. Lori had said her husband was a lawyer. Another coincidence?

He called the number on Costello's business card. As soon as the phone was answered, Fernandez hung up; their office was open.

He walked to the tire store on Orange Avenue, collected his car, and then headed south on U.S. 1 to Costello's office. The address was a rundown storefront.

An attractive, gum-chewing blonde sat behind a desk, filing her nails. "Sal's out of the office."

"When do you expect Mr. Costello back?"

"He didn't say."

"It's important. Can you tell me how to reach him?"

"Mr. Costello's out of the country."

"When is he due back?"

"Who knows?" The woman gave a long, grunting sigh. "I'm just a temp."

Fernandez knew she was lying.

Driving back to his apartment, he wondered if it was Costello who had telephoned him and why the Mafia was warning him off of the Justin Williams case. He thought of Anthony Carlyle's death. The Mafia didn't fuck around. He wondered if there was a connection between Williams and the Mafia.

* * *

RETURNING TO HIS APARTMENT, Fernandez made straight for his desk. He had shredded incriminating papers prior to the FBI visit, but he hadn't destroyed the Justin Williams file or notes made during the interviews following the Carlyle break-in. Fernandez was looking for a connection between Justin Williams and the Mafia.

He knew Williams had taken the Picasso, but he had never been able to establish the motive. Williams hadn't impressed Fernandez as an elitist collector who wished to have exclusive viewing rights to a masterpiece. As director, he worked all day in a museum surrounded by fine art.

He called Garcella Beauvoir.

The hurt in her voice was understandable. "What is it this time, Fernandez? You think I shot President Kennedy? I have an alibi: I was six years old, living in Boston, and I have witnesses."

"I really apologize, Garcella. I was trying to follow the evidence. I ended up flat-out wrong. For that I'm truly sorry. And I always will be."

"Somehow I doubt it. What do you want?"

"Williams' unsolved murder is spooking the art museum's John's Island donors."

"You can't win 'em all," Garcella said. "No suspects, no weapon, no fingerprints, no nothing. I couldn't keep investing resources."

"Help me out here, please. Did you check Williams' finances?"

He heard grumbling and a rustling of papers. "A few years back Williams almost lost his house in a foreclosure. The guy may have known art, but he didn't know beans about finance or real estate. He couldn't make mortgage payments, and the bank lost patience."

Fernandez was taking notes.

"Williams found a foreclosure attorney who helped him keep the property."

"Who was the lawyer?" Fernandez asked, guessing the answer.

"Lawyer named Costello who specialized in mortgages issued by offshore banks. He put Williams into a hard-money refinance loan that carried a big balloon payment due at the end of this year."

Fernandez broke in. "If Williams couldn't come up with the money, he would have lost his house and the suffered the embarrassment of foreclosure."

"You got it. If you find out anything, clue me in."

"That's a promise," Fernandez lied.

He sat at his desk, contemplating the chain of events. If Costello was connected to the DeCavalcante crime family, he knew Anthony Carlyle had tried to foist the fake Picasso in 2012 to repay loans. The Mafia would have employed experts to authenticate the painting. When they realized they'd been conned, they'd arranged to have Anthony Carlyle's boat blown up. But they had never recovered the original Picasso they'd paid for.

He massaged his forehead with both hands. He assumed Williams had planned to use his international contacts to sell the painting and pay off his Mafia debts. And, since Costello was Williams' bankruptcy lawyer, Costello would have knowledge of Williams' intended source of funding to clear up his obligations.

"Aw shit," Fernandez muttered aloud. "That's how the Mafia knew Williams had the authentic Picasso. Then they had him killed and replaced the original in Williams' home with the forgery Carlyle had foisted on them seven years earlier."

Afternoon turned into evening. Evening shaded into night through Fernandez's windows. He sat silently in the darkness for a long time, finally accepting the hard reality: The *Boy with a Pipe* he'd recovered from Lisa Rodriguez's house was a forgery.

Fernandez tapped a number into his phone.

"Quint," he said. "I need to see you."

PART IX

THE FIDDLER

"In the arts, as in life, everything is possible provided it is based on love."
—Marc Chagall

...35

FERNANDEZ WAS ON THE ROAD at 6:30 a.m., gulping coffee as he headed onto the northbound lane of the Florida Turnpike. At the tollbooth he plugged his phone into the charger. For a moment he considered calling Maris, but it was too early to call and maybe too late to repair their slowly dissolving marriage.

*　　*　　*

FERNANDEZ SLUMPED INTO AN OLD rattan chair on Quint Langstaff's patio at the Villages. He exhaled, took a sip of beer, and proceeded to explain everything to the retired FBI art crime investigator, including the Chagall painting. He omitted the tire-slashing incident and the Mafia phone call ultimatum.

"Let me see if I have this straight, Frank. A talented Belgian artist was engaged to forge two copies of Picasso's *Boy with a Pipe*. Then the buyer, a con artist named Anthony Carlyle, switched one of the fake paintings for Jock Whitney's original that was on loan to the museum in Vero Beach. Okay so far?"

"Yeah."

"Good." Langstaff continued, "Carlyle hung the real Picasso in his home and tried to palm off the second forgery to the Mafia to repay shady loans, and for his generous efforts he was bumped off. The first forgery was later auctioned at Sotheby's to a Russian oligarch, who is also no longer with us. Right?"

"Right."

"What happened then?"

"The museum director, Justin Williams, was facing heavy duty mortgage payments due by year end. It took a few days and some unfortunate missteps, but I finally connected the dots: The Mafia got their hooks into Williams by helping him refinance his mortgage. When the Mob demanded their money, Williams was desperate."

"I can guess the rest," Langstaff said. "Williams was the brains behind the break-in during the hurricane. Then he murdered his accomplice and gained possession of Picasso's *Boy with a Pipe*."

"Looks that way," Fernandez said. "The mortgage lawyer was mob-connected. He had to know how and when Williams intended to pay off the debts. Two weeks after the Carlyle robbery, someone murdered Williams in his home, replaced the original Picasso with the fake, and the mob-connected lawyer, Salvadore Costello, disappeared. He's in the wind."

Langstaff grimaced. "Bottom line, the *Boy with a Pipe* in the Vero museum is a forgery."

Fernandez nodded.

"Putting the killing of Justin Williams aside," Langstaff said, "there's perverted justice at play here. The Mafia recovered the artwork they had negotiated for. And, as for the dead Russian, I think the Picasso painting is the least of Putin's concerns. So, what do you want from me, Frank?"

Fernandez pressed his hands against his eyes and drew a deep breath. "There's a lot of shit going down in my life right now. My wife wants to call it quits, and my dad's losing his marbles. What should I do?"

Langstaff gave him a faint smile. "I won't presume to tell you what to do. I'll give you my opinion, that's all. Another beer?"

"No, thanks."

"If you open this can of worms, here's what you can expect to happen: The whole thing will get legal and the museum will sue everybody—including you. Can you afford legal fees?"

"Hardly."

"This puts me in mind of the Matisse theft in Venezuela that I told you about: Matisse's *Odalisque in Red Trousers,* valued at three million dollars.

"It was found in July 2012, when a couple tried to sell it to two of my undercover FBI agents for 740,000 dollars at a hotel in Miami Beach. The real Matisse had been swapped for a copy in 2000, yet the museum's staff and curators, plus thousands of visitors, were unaware of the theft for twelve years. Twelve years, Frank.

"What I learned was, when it comes to art, it's not what people look at that matters; it's what they see. If you do nothing, the painting will be displayed and no one will know the difference, and it will give pleasure to thousands of viewers."

"And when the original surfaces," Fernandez shot back, "then what?"

"Who knows when or even if the original Picasso will ever surface? A lot of these major art deals shun publicity. My advice is to tell *no one* the *Boy with a Pipe* is a forgery. Leave well enough alone, pal. Go home, make nice to the misses, and hope for the best with your dad. They're bringing out new Alzheimer's meds every year."

"It's not that simple, Quint. I never have quit a case. The Riverside Art Museum retained me to investigate the Justin Williams murder—"

Langstaff broke in angrily, "You're not working for the FBI anymore, Fernandez. You can quit any time and drop the Williams investigation. The guy was a murderer, a thief and a pedophile. Fuck him. But there's part of you that can't let go, can you? You're a dreamer. People who can't separate dreams from reality need professional help. I advise you to get it."

Langstaff had hit a raw nerve.

"Maybe I will," Fernandez lied.

* * *

BEFORE LEAVING THE VILLAGES, he pulled into a McDonald's drive-thru for a quick snack and coffee. Sitting in the parking lot munching a cheeseburger, he mulled over the situation. Regardless of Langstaff's advice, Fernandez felt morally obligated to update Garcella Beauvoir. He didn't want her blindsided if the original Picasso surfaced.

Garcella picked up on the first ring.

"When we were at Fisherman's Wharf," Fernandez began, "you told me to keep you informed of everything I found. Not crumbs, everything."

Her voice sounded strange. "Yes. I did."

"There are some things you need to know." He cleared his throat. "The Picasso painting I delivered to you last Saturday … was not the original. It was a forgery. I had no idea. The original is in the hands of a Mafia lawyer named Costello, who is now off the grid."

Fernandez was surprised when Garcella made no response. He took a breath. "It was the Mafia who arranged the hit on Justin Williams."

There was a long pause.

He heard Garcella sigh. "Thank you for sharing the information." Her voice hardened. "And thanks to you, I missed visiting with my mother last Tuesday."

"I told you how sorry I—"

Garcella cut him off. "I *did* manage to get to see her today—at her funeral. My mother died of a heart attack last Tuesday night." Her voice broke. "I should have been with her. I thought there would be time, but we always think stuff like that. Don't we?"

Fernandez felt himself mist up.

...36

DRIVING TIME FROM THE VILLAGES to St. Petersburg was just under two hours. Passing through the town of Rital, Fernandez ran into heavy weather. Lightning crashed overhead, and heavy rain lashed against his windshield. He had difficulty seeing the road and swerved across the yellow line. A truck horn blared, and he didn't blame the driver for the middle finger that flashed. It had been a near collision.

The conversation with Garcella had unsettled Fernandez. He barely noticed when the storm faded to a few flashes of lightning and faint rumbles somewhere over the Florida panhandle.

He also wanted to avoid a confrontation with Maris. They had tried reconciliation, again and again. Their attempts at reunion were always dashed by his unwillingness to give up investigative work.

At five p.m., Fernandez arrived at Maris's apartment. When she answered the door, he noticed she still used a cane. He held both hands up. "I'm sorry. Please, let's talk. After that, if you want me to leave, I will."

"What do you want, Frank?"

He cleared his throat. "Tell me about your physical problem."

"I need knee surgery to repair a torn meniscus, but I've been putting it off."

"Why?"

"Who is going to take care of Charlie? Tell me," she snapped. "You? You've never shouldered the role of father, and you nearly got my child kidnapped."

Fernandez tried to ignore her outburst. "How long is the recovery period?"

"After surgery, I'll be on crutches for a week or so." Maris paused. "They offered me the job as director of the Riverside Museum. I'm going to turn it down. I'm not sure I want to move again."

"Where is Charlie?"

"Sleeping."

"Can I take a peep?"

Charlie lay in bed squirming and whimpering, his brow furrowed.

"Don't cry, son. You're going to be okay."

The boy arched his back and opened his eyes but didn't speak. Then Charlie lowered his head, and after a while he was snoring softly.

Fernandez rearranged the blanket over him and gave his forehead a kiss.

He joined Maris in the living room. She looked wary.

"While you're in the hospital, I'll look after Charlie."

"No way, Frank." Her eyes were blazing. "You've made promises before. I won't sacrifice my son on the altar of your quixotic neurosis. I guess you have to prove you have as big a prick as your war hero father, but—"

Fernandez held up a hand. "Hold it. My war hero father, as we speak, is in a Baltimore nursing home suffering from dementia. Yesterday, Dad wheeled himself out on the sidewalk hollering to people to save him, he was being held as a prisoner of war."

"I'm sorry. I didn't know."

"You are the only family I have, Maris. What do I have to do?"

Maris paled, her lips nearly gray. "My father taught me trust was like an icicle—once it melted, that was the end of it. I don't trust you anymore, Frank.

"Go away. Please, go away. Leave us alone."

...37

SATURDAY MORNING FERNANDEZ slept late. He roused himself and looked at his watch. It was half past ten. He felt sluggish and sore, conscious of a dull ache in his chest. In the bathroom, he caught sight of himself in the mirror, crumpled-looking and unshaven. The lines around his eyes were deep and earned. He allowed himself a smile thinking of Maris calling him a quixotic neurotic. His mind drifted. At an age when anyone with sense slowed down, took up golf or bought a boat, he felt hollowed out. Alone.

Fernandez flopped down heavily on the living room sofa and put his arms over the top of his head. He loved Maris and Charlie. What worried him was the practical side. If he gave up his investigation business, what would he do? His FBI pension barely covered current living expenses, and his social security wouldn't kick in for years. Even if Maris accepted the new job, he wasn't sure they could afford a house and Charlie's education.

He lay there idly staring at the painting on the wall. Avram Markus had explained that Marc Chagall's artwork depicted life as a balancing act; a precarious journey filled with challenges. "Cherish your family," Avram had written in his letter. "I speak from sad experience. In the end, family is all we have."

On a whim he got up, lifted the painting off the wall and flipped it over. In the lower right corner on the back of the canvas, he caught sight of scrawled handwriting:

To Avram,

In the arts, as in life, everything is possible provided it is based on love.

Marc Chagall, Paris 1963

Fernandez tilted his head, narrowed his eyes, and studied the Chagall painting again. He booted up his computer and Googled "Current value Marc Chagall original oil painting, Fiddler series."

When he read the information, Fernandez let out a long, slow whistle. He tapped in "How to Open an Offshore Bank Account in Cayman Islands."

* * *

BY NOON, FERNANDEZ HAD COMPLETED five important telephone calls. His final call was to his wife. Again, Fernandez got her answering machine.

"Maris," he said. "It's probably best to be direct. I hired Anthony from Beachfront Mann Realty to find us a house; I notified my landlord that I was going out of business; I told that bitch from the Riverside Museum to go fuck herself; and I accepted the teaching slot at Indian River College."

He paused. "And, oh yes. I booked hotel and flight reservations for you, Charlie and me to vacation in the Cayman Islands.

"And one more thing, honey. If I don't get an affirmative return call from you, I'm taking Janice.

"Love you. Bye."

...38

THREE MONTHS LATER Quint Langstaff was surfing the Internet. A notice appeared in *The Art Newspaper,* an online publication based in London and New York covering news and developments in the art world.

> A 1913 masterpiece, *The Fiddler* by Marc Chagall, commanded an exceptional price of US $4 million (HK $32,172,000), becoming the most expensive painting by a modern western artist ever sold at an auction in Asia. The quasi-cubist painting is a representation of a fiddler in Chagall's village, Vitebsk. *The Fiddler* was sold by an anonymous seller, who was represented by an offshore bank on the Cayman Islands.
>
> —*South China Morning Post.* International edition

Langstaff stared at the screen for a moment, then took another long look and shook his head.

"God damn," he said, smiling.

PART X

BOY WITH A PIPE

"The purpose of art is washing
the dust of daily life off our souls."
—Pablo Picasso

...39

IN JANUARY, THE NEW SEMESTER began at Indian River State College. The sale of the Chagall painting had provided Fernandez with financial independence, but he had accepted the teaching job to fulfill a pledge to Maris and provide something to do with his time.

He nervously riffled through his notes, took a deep breath, exhaled and began.

"Good morning, ladies and gentlemen. My name is Mr. Fernandez. This semester we will cover a practical introduction to criminal investigations, including the fundamentals of proper evidence handling, law enforcement techniques and interrogation.

"We will also cover recent technological changes, such as computerized print technology, the specificity of DNA, and the expanding sources of metadata that reveal linkages of previously unknown suspects to crimes they committed. These techniques assist the investigator in being prepared, focused, objective and successful in obtaining the truth.

"For many years I served with the FBI. I will try to teach you how to follow established protocols, but most people only learn from experience. I've learned that experience can be the worst teacher, because she gives the test first and the lessons afterwards."

Touching his chest, he added, "Learning is not compulsory. Neither is survival, and I've got two bullet slugs lodged next to my heart to prove it."

Students put aside their mobile devices. Fernandez had their attention.

He noticed a pretty blonde in the first row, her generously freckled breasts barely contained in the pink deep V-neck low-cut blouse.

She gave him an inviting smile while crossing her legs, moving one caressingly against the other. Fernandez observed she was apparently not wearing underwear.

He gripped the podium, took a deep breath and tried to refocus. "My chest injuries resulted from a failed FBI drug bust in a Miami whorehouse—I m-m-mean w-w-warehouse," he stammered.

The class thought Fernandez was injecting a little humor into his presentation. They responded with a warm round of applause for their new instructor.

...40

FERNANDEZ THOUGHT OF LISA RODRIGUEZ and her family in Puerto Rico as he read the *New York Times* editorial headlined "Hurricanes Wreak Havoc on Puerto Rico."

> From a meteorological standpoint, Irma and Maria were a worst-case scenario for the territory: The center of a huge, nearly Category 5 hurricane, Maria made a direct hit on Puerto Rico, lashing the island with wind and rain for longer than 30 hours, causing a level of widespread destruction and disorganization paralleled by few storms in American history. Most of the island's residents still lack access to electricity, food and clean water.

He picked up the phone, called his contact at Oculina Bank, and authorized the withdrawal of a large amount to be sent to Lisa Rodriguez anonymously in the form of a cashier's check.

The same week, the Indian River Art Gallery in Fort Pierce announced construction plans for a new wing to be dedicated to Highwaymen artwork: paintings by self-taught African-American landscape artists, mostly from the Fort Pierce area, who originally peddled their work from the trunks of their cars along A1A and U.S. 1. An anonymous donor provided the funding for the new addition.

...41

ON FEBRUARY 6TH, FERNANDEZ RECEIVED a call from his brother.

"It's ... Dad," Martin said.

Fernandez had dreaded the call. A wave of guilt washed over him. He wished with all his heart he had kept his promise to visit his father. Now he feared he would never see Luis again.

"Tell me."

He heard his brother chuckle. "North Oaks is threatening to expel our father. I just received a letter from their attorney. It seems Dad is visiting female residents in their rooms in the middle of the night."

Fernandez exhaled with relief.

"While none of the ladies are complaining, Dad's behavior violates the facility's rules and regulations. The administrator is concerned about code violations and legal liability. The letter was a warning that if Dad doesn't stop his 'night rounds,' he's out."

"Jesus, Martin. What should we do?"

"I gave Dad two large bags of licorice today. The main compound in licorice candy is glycyrrhizic acid, which decreases testosterone. If that doesn't work, we'll mix sleeping pills in his night meds.

"You have any thoughts?" Martin asked.

"Yeah. No more licorice for me."

* * *

GARCELLA BEAUVOIR forwarded to Fernandez a copy of an article from the *Yucatan Times* dated April 7, 2018. Pinned to the Mexican newspaper was a note: "FYI."

> This morning Mexican authorities announced the grim slaying of Fort Pierce, Florida attorney Mr. Salvadore Costello at his vacation home in Cancun. Mexican police officials believe the killing resulted from an art-for-drugs swap turned lethal. Rumors circulated that Mr. Costello was negotiating the exchange of a valuable work of art for cocaine. According to Mexican Attorney General Raul Esparza, "In Mexico, art crime is the third highest-grossing criminal trade, just behind drugs and weapons." Mrs. Costello, the victim's widow, returned to her parents' home in New Jersey.

Fernandez wondered if the original *Boy with a Pipe* would ever surface again.

When his iPhone chirped, he saw it was Lou Brumberg calling. He was tempted to let it go to voice mail, but curiosity and old habits caused him to pick up.

"What's up, Lou?"

"Just wanted you to know that Chief Warrant Officer Leroy Martin's picture has been added to our wall of honor in the SEAL Museum."

"Thanks for the call. I appreciate it. By the way, how's Vinnie DeCicco?"

"Strange you should ask. I thought Vinnie loved the Florida climate and fishing, but he's listed his unit for sale. Vinnie's moving back north. Told me he was getting older and wanted to be near his family."

"In Elizabeth, New Jersey?"

"How the hell did you know that, Frank?"
"I'm a—I used to be a detective."

...42

THE CONTROVERSY OVER THE LEGAL custodianship of *Boy with a Pipe* continued. Vladimir Tsurikov, director of the Museum of Russian Art, stated, "We entered legal action having been left with no recourse after the Riverside Art Museum refused to return the artwork or repay the 104 million dollars Grisha Chuychenko originally paid Sotheby's for the Picasso painting."

Lawyers for the Riverside Art Museum argued *caveat emptor,* that it was the buyer's responsibility for due diligence before making the purchase and therefore the Museum of Russian Art had no legal claim on *Boy with a Pipe.*

Meanwhile, in Vero Beach, the Picasso masterpiece was drawing record crowds to the Riverside Art Museum. When the annual meeting of the American Association of University Women was scheduled for Vero Beach, the museum visit topped their agenda.

Executive Director Maris Fernandez conducted the women on their tour. At the Picasso masterpiece, the group huddled around Maris.

"*Boy with a Pipe* was painted in 1905," she said, "when Picasso lived in the Montmartre section of Paris. The year was a transition year for Picasso. His palette was changing from the cold and depressive colors of the blue period into the warm and joyful colors of the rose period. It was during this period that the twenty-four-year-old Picasso painted this masterpiece, which is one of his greatest portrait paintings.

"One of the reasons we love art is because it strikes a visceral chord in us, and I think you will agree *Boy with a*

Pipe offers such a simple and rigorous beauty that it commands your gaze and thoughts … and emotions."

"If you look closely, ladies, you will notice that the face of little Louis, the ten-year-old Parisian model, has an unblemished white look, in contrast with his worn, dirty overalls. By adding the garland of flowers in the background, Picasso transformed the painting into something lyrical and beautiful.

"In this manner the artist expresses his belief that the purpose of art is to wash the dust of daily life off of our souls."

A woman raised her hand. "I was brought up, like so many in my generation, to idolize Picasso. But wasn't there a dark side to his genius?"

Maris's face relaxed into a fleeting smile. "The man was an egomaniacal womanizer who thought all women were goddesses or doormats. He was also the obsessive genius who produced over 13,000 paintings, in addition to thousands of prints, sculptures and ceramics. He may have been a son of a bitch—but love him or hate him, Pablo Picasso was the most important artist of the twentieth century."

...43

THE DOORBELL RANG at Fernandez's new home. The UPS driver asked him to sign for a small package from overseas—Israel. The only person Fernandez knew with connections to Israel was Avram Markus.

While Charlie sat mutely on the sofa watching TV reruns of *Little Einsteins,* Fernandez snipped open the packet. Inside was a small glassine envelope containing a gold medallion.

Fernandez recognized the gold medal: the Distinguished Intelligence Cross, awarded by the CIA for voluntary acts of extraordinary heroism. Accompanying the medal was a letter.

Dear Mr. Fernandez,

It is with sadness I inform you that Avram Markus has died. Avram was my oldest friend and army comrade in our elite Israeli commando unit *Savret Matkal.*

Years ago, Avram met a beautiful Druid Muslim girl named Sarai from a border village near our kibbutz in the Jezreel Valley. Against his family's urgings, Avram married his love and lived in our kibbutz. A year later they had a baby boy, Zak.

At the time, Avram was lecturer at the Mossad training facility. Our class was interrupted by a visit from Prime Minister Shamir.

Shamir informed Avram that terrorists had ambushed an army patrol. Three Israeli soldiers were killed. In trying to target enemy rocket launchers, Israeli artillery fired short rounds that accidentally struck the Lebanese town of Ghajar, Avram's wife's village. On that day Sarai and Zak were visiting her family. They were both killed.

Shamir feared if news of the army's ineptness hit the papers, his government might not hold together. He ordered a news blackout and ordered Avram to remain silent about the event that had killed the two most important people in his life.

My best friend honored the prime minister's request, but resigned his commission, left Israel, and immigrated to the United States.

Before his death, Avram charged me to carry out his last wishes; his body was buried in our kibbutz cemetery beside his beloved Sarai and Zak. Avram also entrusted me to forward the enclosed medallion to you—his American son.

Sincerely,
General Marcus Loeb

Fernandez felt drained of thought and energy, like a stone was lodged in his heart. He opened his desk drawer and removed the letter Avram had attached to the Chagall painting. The final lines read:

> *There are few emotional investments a man can make in his life like the one he makes in a son, whether that son carries his DNA or not. We shall not see each other again. Remember me.*

Charlie wiggled off the sofa and crawled onto his lap. The boy's arms encircled Fernandez's neck. In a small voice he murmured, "Take care of me, Poppie."

As Fernandez heard Charlie speak for the first time, tears rolled down his cheeks. He tried to swipe them away with the back of his hand.

He reflected on Avram Markus's advice: "Cherish your family, my dear Mr. Fernandez. I speak from sad experience. In the end, family is all we have."

Fernandez touched his son's sweaty forehead and kissed his cheek. "I'll take care of you, little guy," he said. "I promise I will."

ACKNOWLEDGMENTS

LET'S BE HONEST: it would make sense to steer clear of an acknowledgments page, and instead give the readers, editor and graphic designer a bottle of wine, a thank you and a copy of the book.

But that somehow doesn't cut it, because I've been helped immeasurably. So thank you Gene Hull, Eugene Schreiber and Dana and Dr. Jeff Dobson for giving generously of your time and valued suggestions.

And thanks to my son Scott for the graphics and to Jennifer Adkins for editing with a calm professionalism that keeps me sane, on point, and forever grateful.

Also my appreciation to Highwayman artist Willie Daniels for permission to use *Poinciana Tree*. And to Gisela Fabian for allowing use of *Revenge*, by Riguad Benoit, one of the most influential names in Haitian art.

Writing is a lonely job. Having people who believe in you makes a world of difference. For those wonderful folks who stop by on Saturday mornings at the Fort Pierce Market and say, "When's your next book coming out?"

I'm on it. THANKS.

Other books by Malcolm Mahr you will enjoy:

The Secret Diary of Marco Polo

Two grisly murders are inextricably linked to the past. The body of a Venetian mu-seum curator is found floating in the Grand Canal. Five thousand miles away, the body of a CIA operative is found float-ing in the Ft. Pierce Inlet. The legendary agent code-named The Venetian was the 34th and last descendant of Venice's greatest son, Marco Polo.

The Return of the Scorpion

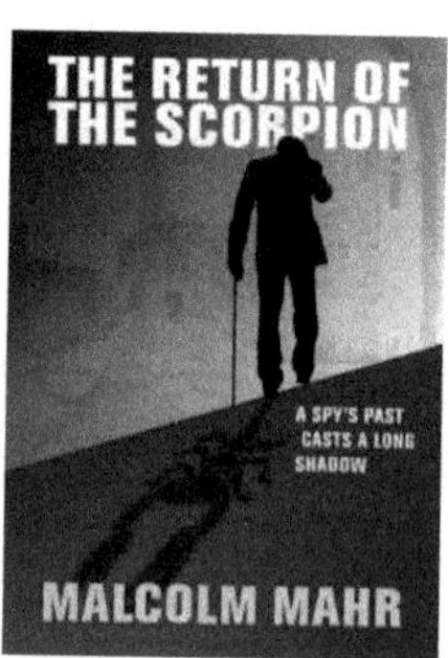

A spy's past casts a long shadow. In Fort Pierce, Florida, a former CIA operative, code-named Scorpion, is living under an as-sumed identity. Against his will, the Scor-pion is summoned back to the Agency and dispatched on an urgent mission he cannot refuse, to a place called Armageddon.

Murder at the Paradise Spa

A bestial murder occurs in a fashionable Palm Beach spa. Blood on the wall; owl feathers on the floor. The police are baf-fled. It falls to retired psychologist Maxwell Wolfe, with the help of his wife Millie, to work their way through this macabre mystery.

FRANK FERNANDEZ MYSTERY SERIES

The Orange Blossom Mob

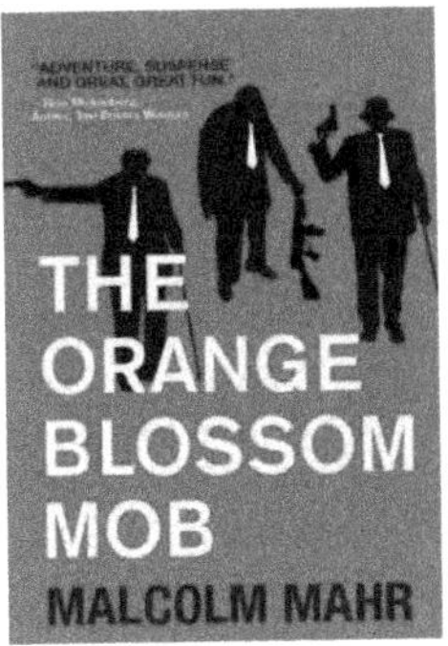

Five geriatric mobsters retire to Florida and volunteer their special talents to aid police in lowering the crime rate.

The Einstein Project

In Jerusalem, an American is murdered. Two days earlier, in the Arabian Sea an eerie bolt of lightning struck an Israeli warship. An Islamic terrorist group claimed responsibility. Former FBI agent Frank Fernandez delves deeper into the two mysteries, leading to a shocking scientific discovery and a conspiracy of staggering brilliance.

The Hostage

The President asks retired FBI agent Frank Fernandez to investigate the dis-appearance of her elderly mother from a Fort Pierce nursing facility. Fernan-dez can trust no one as he tries to dis-cover who is behind the plot to destabi-lize the American Presidency.

Available in paperback & Kindle •
www.malcolmmahr.com

The Golden Madonna

On July 29th, 1715, the treasure fleet of Spanish King Philip V left Cuba and sailed into history. While navigating the Florida Straits, the armada was struck by a violent hurricane. All eleven galleons were destroyed. Millions in gold, silver and jewelry were scattered on the reefs and sands off the Florida coast. More than 700 people perished in one of the worst sea disasters of all time. Over the years, treasure salvagers swapped tales of sunken fortunes. Veiled in myth, one story dealt with a life-sized gold statue of a Madonna and Christ Child. Ex-FBI agent Frank Fernandez is called upon to investigate the merciless murder of two treasure hunters who were searching for the Golden Madonna.

No Man's Land

In 1915, Germany launched an offensive against the Ypres salient, a bulge in the Allied lines in Belgium. The Canadian 1st Division valiantly defended this po-sition, but they paid a high price: 6,000 casualties over the four-day battle. In this historical fiction an Ameri-can joined the Canadian Army seeking glory and ex-citement. What Christopher Campbell encountered was the bloody slaughter pits of Ypres and the dark waters of politics.

In 2015, a Belgium farmer uncovered bones buried in a makeshift mud grave. Campbell's remains were identified by his I.D. disc and West Point ring. Foren-sics indicated the man had been murdered—under strange circumstances. Christopher Campbell's family turns to former FBI Agent Frank Fernandez to inves-tigate this bizarre 100-year-old cold case.

Sandbag Castle

A novel inspired by true events.The murder of a Korean War veteran exposed a malignant injustice never forgotten from the Forgotten War.

The Da Vinci Deception

Before his death in 1517, Leonardo DaVinci devised an inspired stratagem to preserve his nude mas-ter-work *Monna Vanna* from being destroyed by the pow-erful arch-conservative forces of *de l'inquisition*. Five centuries later, an American art professor, Dov Mar-kov, embarks on a dangerous search for the lost Da Vinci painting. Markov must confront ruthless international art traffickers, the Russian Mafia, and a secret religious sect known as the Order of the Sword of St. Jerome—the "Holy Madmen."

Murder by the Numbers—
Due Fall 2019

Available in paperback & Kindle •
www.malcolmmahr.com

CPSIA information can be obtained
at www.ICGtesting.com
Printed in the USA
FSHW011947200219
55822FS

9 780692 197516